D0627806

Indira realized too late that she had been a fool to climb the outcrop of rock. How many times had Conrad warned everyone not to take chances? She, a veteran Expendable, should have known that she should have concentrated on her assigned task.

The cloud of piranha bugs she spied was a large one. It hung above the hovercar as if trying to make up its collective mind what the strange thing was.

Indira thought rapidly. If she could get to the car and get inside it, she would be all right. But she had grounded the vehicle more than a hundred meters from the outcrop.

THE KILLER BUGS WERE FAST. SHE KNEW SHE HAD TO BE FASTER. . . .

Fawcett Gold Medal Books
by Richard Avery:

THE EXPENDABLES

#1 THE DEATHWORMS OF KRATOS

#2 THE RINGS OF TANTALUS

#3 THE WAR GAMES OF ZELOS

#4 THE VENOM OF ARGUS

ARE THERE FAWCETT PAPERBACKS
YOU WANT BUT CANNOT FIND IN YOUR LOCAL STORES?

You can get any title in print in Fawcett Crest, Fawcett Premier, or Fawcett Gold Medal editions. Simply send title and retail price, plus 50¢ for book postage and handling for the first book and 25¢ for each additional book, to:

MAIL ORDER DEPARTMENT,
FAWCETT PUBLICATIONS,
P.O. Box 1014
GREENWICH, CONN. 06830

There is no charge for postage and handling on orders for five books or more.

Books are available at discounts in quantity lots for industrial or sales-promotional use. For details write FAWCETT WORLD LIBRARY, CIRCULATION MANAGER, FAWCETT BLDG., GREENWICH, CONN. 06830

THE EXPENDABLES #4

The Venom Of Argus

Richard Avery

A FAWCETT GOLD MEDAL BOOK

Fawcett Publications, Inc., Greenwich, Connecticut

THE EXPENDABLES #4

THE VENOM OF ARGUS

Copyright © 1976 by Richard Avery

All rights reserved, including the right to reproduce this book or portions thereof in any form.

ISBN 0-449-13586-1

All characters in this book are fictitious, and any resemblance to actual persons living or dead is purely coincidental.

Printed in the United States of America

10   9   8   7   6   5   4   3   2   1

CONTENTS

Stage One

Prelude to Argus

Phase One

Rumpus

Commander James Conrad had to pass a lot of security guards to get into the ExPEND building and up to the Director's suite on the twenty-fifth floor. But he did not have to show his ID card. Everyone knew the man with the silver patch over his right eye.

It had been deemed necessary to give the Extra-Solar Planets Evaluating and Normalizing Department top security two or three years ago. Some misguided Third World fanatic had managed to get through the normal security net and dump about twenty litres of nitro-glycerine in the basement with the apparent aim of putting the Director and his staff in orbit. He was frustrated in his ambition only because of an electronics failure in the timed detonator. When the ExPEND building failed to go boom according to plan, he came back to investigate. By that time the nitro had been discovered and a reception committee was waiting for him. Since then security was tighter than for an atomics plant.

As Conrad had stepped out of his hovercar, the external duty officer—resplendent in his neatly pressed U.N. uniform—took one glance and snapped out the order: "Present arms!"

Ten men pointed their laser rifles at the sky and slapped the butts and simultaneously, eyes front, becoming motionless as statues.

Conrad was embarrassed. His rank did not qualify him for that kind of treatment. He approached the duty officer and fumbled in his pocket for the ID card.

"Sir, identification is not necessary."

"Dammit, man, I could be a bloody fake!" said Conrad testily.

The duty officer permitted himself a nervous smile. "With respect, no, sir. We have already dealt with two fake Conrads. We know the real article. We were expecting you. I believe your appointment with the Director is for fourteen thirty."

"It is."

With remarkable speed, the duty officer produced a photograph of Conrad.

"Sir, I have a small son who would be———"

"I have no sons—or daughters," said Conrad. "How old is your boy?"

"Seven, sir."

"What is his name?"

"James Conrad Kennedy." The duty officer held out a stylo. "If you would sign the photograph, sir, he would treasure it to the end of his days."

"What does the boy want to do with his life?"

The duty officer smiled. "He wants to become an Expendable, sir."

"Then tell him that Expendables are no damn good. They are misfits, criminals and bums. If you will agree to enter him for the U.N. Space Service, I will sign."

"Agreed, sir."

Conrad wrote: Best wishes to James Conrad Kennedy from plain James Conrad. "Is he a bright boy?" He gave the photo and stylo back to the officer.

The officer glanced at the message. "Sir, thank you. Young Conrad will be over the hill with pride about this . . . Yes, sir, he's a bright boy. Grade One in maths. He is already into elementary astrophysics."

From out of nowhere, a couple of vid men had appeared, cameras rolling. Somebody must have tipped off the gentlemen of the media. Conrad scratched his silver patch irritably and sighed. It was always like this, now, when he was back on Terra. He couldn't even go into a bar and finish his first drink before the vids started rolling. He would be glad to get back into space once more.

"Then tell the young one that the old one wishes to see another Conrad in the Space Service . . . And get your men to stop looking like statues." He gestured towards the vid men. "Also, if you can remove these gentlemen, I would be grateful."

The officer saluted. "Sir! Yes, sir!"

Conrad hurried into the ExPEND building. He had to return half a dozen salutes before he reached the twenty-fifth floor.

The time was fourteen twenty-eight. Conrad still took some pride in being punctual.

The Director's secretary was a bosomy blonde. Very sexy. Human secretaries were a sign of very high status these days. Most people made do with robosecs.

"Good afternoon, Commander. The Director is expecting you, of course, but at the moment he is heavily engaged. As soon as he is free, I will——"

Conrad interrupted her. "Which means he is not yet back from lunch, I suppose. Otherwise, you would have signalled my arrival."

The secretary neither confirmed nor denied. She stuck out her breasts. Diversion number one. Then offered a drink. Diversion number two.

Conrad declined to consider either breasts or drink. Also he declined the offer of a very comfortable chair. He went to the window and gazed out over the city.

London had changed greatly since he had last seen it. Was that before Zelos or Tantalus or Kratos? He couldn't really remember and he didn't really want to know. Where Buckingham Palace had once stood, the United Europe Tower, with its one hundred storeys, rose like a glass and hiduminium phallus towards the sky. Where the National Gallery had been there was the Data Processing Centre of the U.N.S.S. But the church of St. Martin-in-the-Fields still survived, and that was something. Not that Conrad was religious. He hated superstition of every kind. But he loved old buildings.

"The Director will see you now, Commander."

Conrad went into the Director's luxuriously appointed office and gazed round him disapprovingly.

"I hope I didn't keep you waiting too long, Commander Conrad."

"Six minutes," said Conrad, leaving the other man to work out if that was too long.

"Please sit down, Conrad. We have much to discuss."

So now he was just plain Conrad. "Thank you—sir," he said managing to get a hint of irony into the final word.

The Director was a fat, balding man in his late fifties—a career politician who always seized the main chance. Conrad knew his track record. Chairborne in the U.N.S.S. Administration for fifteen years, chairborne in U.N. for about ten years, and now chairborne in ExPEND. But he had once held the rank of commodore in U.N.S.S. so, presumably, some other chairborne wonder had thought he knew something about space.

"I want to discuss with you the modifications you have suggested for the new F.T.L. vessel now in design stage. Apart from the engine-room modifications which seem sensible and which I, as Director, have approved, there are certain other suggested changes which appear to be somewhat unnecessary and which would, if accepted, cost a great deal of money. For example, you suggest a larger, reinforced landing torus. Why? The one on the *Santa Maria* has proved adequate for three missions."

"It is easily damaged," explained Conrad. "The safety of the vessel depends on the strength of the torus. We had some damage on Kratos. It wasn't critical. But with a large diameter torus, suitably strengthened, we would not be so restricted in our choice of touch-down areas."

The Director gazed coldly at Conrad. "The new design you have submitted would cost—I am told—an additional three point seven five million solars, apart from R and D costs. This is not acceptable."

"Why is it not acceptable—sir?"

"Because of our restricted budget, man! You deep-space cowboys don't seem to know what is going on back here on Earth. U.N. has fiscal problems, so ExPEND has fiscal problems. Terra's natural resources are almost exhausted."

"I know. That is why we deep-space cowboys are busy proving new worlds where nobody will have fiscal problems for a very long time . . . And how many billion solars did you lose on the Janus mission, Director?"

"That is not the point!" thundered the Director. "The Janus mission failed because——"

"Because," interrupted Conrad, "one of those bloody clever S.P.10 robots that are supposed to be capable of making value judgments and acting independently made the wrong value judgment."

There was a brief silence. For a moment or two, the Director looked thunderstruck. Then he recovered himself. "Commander Conrad, the cause of the Janus disaster is at present classified Most Secret. Unless your statement is mere conjecture, I must ask you to reveal your source of information."

Conrad rewarded him with a wintry smile. "Don't go stupid on me—sir. Expendables are trained to find out what they need to know. It's a necessary survival skill."

The Director suddenly realized he was being made to look silly. "Conrad, I order you to withdraw the claim or reveal your source of information. I will not tolerate ——"

"What you will not tolerate doesn't interest me." snapped Conrad. "I have spent part of my precious leave attending four funerals—one in Russia, one in France, one in Cuba and one in Israel. I didn't see you at any of them. I wonder why."

"Conrad, this interview is terminated! I will assume— charitably—that you have been drinking. I shall require to receive a written apology for your extraordinary attitude, or your letter of resignation. Otherwise, I shall be compelled to dismiss you from the service."

"Director, this interview is not yet terminated. I didn't know Yuri Litvinov too well. I only met him at the briefing sessions. But we liked each other, and he played a mean game of chess. But the others were my personal friends. Chantana Le Gros and Fidel Batista were with me on Kratos. Ruth Zonis, as you may recall, took some rough treatment on Tantalus . . . These were *my* people, Director. When they died. I wanted to know how and why they died. I found out."

The Director pressed a button on his communications

console. "Miss Angstrom, Commander Conrad is unwell and in a highly excited state. Have two security guards escort him from the building. Also arrange for a psychiatric examination."

A shocked intake of breath was audible. "Willco, Director. Instantly."

Conrad leaned back in his chair. "Director, you disappoint me. Just in case you didn't know—which doesn't seem likely—I'll tell you what happened on Janus."

At that moment, two security guards burst into the office. They carried laser rifles at the ready. Their eyes were popping with amazement.

"Escort Commander Conrad out," said the Director. "He is in a distressed condition. Stay with him and be prepared to restrain him, if necessary, until the ambulance arrives."

"Gentlemen," said Conrad tranquilly, "do I look as if I'm in a distressed condition? I merely want to tell the Director some things he doesn't really want to know. Then I will leave peaceably. That is a promise."

"Sir," said one of the guards hesitantly, "we have orders to remove you."

Conrad stood up. "I appreciate your problem. But I'm not going just yet. I'll go peaceably, in five minutes. You have my word."

"Remove him *now!*" said the Director. "That is an order."

The guards were very unhappy. One said to the Director: "Sir, with great respect, will you allow Commander Conrad five more minutes of your time? It would be easier all round."

"He leaves now. And when this incident is over, report to me for disciplinary action. I will not tolerate my orders being questioned."

The guard shrugged. "I'm sorry, Commander. You'd better come with us. Maybe you can talk to the Director some other time."

Conrad shook his head. The laser rifles were pointing at his chest. "Gentlemen, I hate to put you in this position; but it is important that I talk to the Director." He pointed

14

to the rifles. "If you are going to burn me, you had better do it quickly. I don't like being on the wrong end of those things."

One of the guards threw his rifle down in disgust. "Hell, Commander, you know we can't burn you. We are just going to have to take you by main force."

"I'm sorry about that," said Conrad. "No hard feelings, I hope?"

"No hard feelings, sir."

The other guard put his rifle down. Keeping their eyes on Conrad, both of them advanced cautiously.

He waited until they were about to rush him, then he stepped forward and struck with lightning speed. The prosthetic hand became a fist. It seemed to lightly brush the chin of one guard. As it did so, Conrad swung his body; and, almost without hesitation the fist connected with the other guard's chin. Both men dropped simultaneously. Conrad whirled and saw that the Director was about to call for reinforcements. The prosthetic hand continued its arc of movement and came down to smash the intercom.

Conrad relaxed.

"Now, Director. We'll talk."

"This is the end of the road for you, Conrad," said the Director furiously. "I'll see that you never obtain another command."

Conrad ignored him. "Yuri Litvinov asked my opinion about the S.P.10 robots. I told him what I thought—that a robot that will obey any lawful command without hesitation is more reliable than a fancy piece of hardware that is supposed to make up its own mind what to do in a crisis."

He glanced at the Director, who now stared at him like a rabbit mesmerized by a snake. "*My* robots—Matthew and the rest of the S.P.9s—have a good track record. They functioned perfectly on Kratos, Tantalus and Zelos."

The Director vainly tried to recover his wits. "You lost some, Conrad."

"I know. My fault, not theirs . . . Yuri told me he would settle for the S.P.9s. Then you brainwashed him or blackmailed him into taking S.P.10s to Janus . . . And

15

what happened? He got himself stuck in a quicksand, having been bitten by some kind of land crab already identified, analysed and on the lethal list. He knew he was dying, Director. So he told S.P.10/1 to go back and warn Zonis, who was about a hundred metres behind him in the forest . . ."

Conrad brought his prosthetic hand down on the Director's desk and smashed a hole through the thick oak top.

"But that bloody robot decided to play God! It told itself that Yuri was more important than Ruth because he was the Bossman. So it saved a dying man and then went back for Ruth. Full marks! It found her and they took Yuri back to the *Golden Hinde*. What nobody discovered until it was too late was that fleas from the land crab had also settled on Yuri . . ."

Conrad smashed another hole in the desk. "By making its own value judgment, that bloody robot brought about the deaths of all seven Expendables. The crab fleas carried a bacillus similar to that which caused the Black Death on Terra in the fourteenth century. Only this one was more virulent. Once aboard the *Golden Hinde,* it managed to wipe the Expendables out in less than four days. So then those goddam robots put all the bodies in the cooler, terminated the mission and brought the *Golden Hinde* back."

"How do you know all this?" asked the now terrified Director weakly.

Conrad gave him a thin smile. "One of the privileges of being famous, Director, is that you find you have close friends you have never even heard of. I talked to the robots, I read the *Golden Hinde*'s log, and I got copies of the autopsy reports . . . I also discovered that you have a financial interest in Self-Programming Robots Incorporated. And how do you like that?"

"Conrad, if you are hinting that——"

"I am not hinting, Director—sir. I'm telling you . . . When any of *my* people die, I want to know the reason. I've found it. I don't like you, I don't like the way you operate, and I didn't like attending funerals in four different countries . . . I don't care what you do to me, you bastard, but this message comes to you from Ruth Zonis, Chantana Le Gros, Fidel Batista and Yuri Litvinov with love."

Conrad leaned over the desk, put out his prosthetic arm, grabbed the Director by his lapels and lifted him clean out of his chair.

"You are going to need new teeth, Director, sir, because some of those you already have, you are about to swallow."

He struck with his bio-arm. Oddly, he wanted to feel the pain as his knuckles smashed into the fat man's mouth.

"One for Ruth!" The first blow squashed the Director's lips. Blood oozed.

"One for Chantana!" The second blow smashed the lips back into the teeth. The Director struggled feebly, gurgling; but Conrad's prosthetic hand held him firmly.

"One for Fidel!" The Director's face was now a mess. He was only semi-conscious.

"And one for Yuri!" Conrad felt the pain and was glad of it as his bio-fist knocked teeth out of the Director's top and bottom jaw.

The Director was now coughing, spitting blood, fragments of teeth, fragments of bone.

Conrad dragged him over the desk. "Think yourself lucky you are still living. Director, sir. If you wish to prefer charges when you come out of the hospital, I will be available."

Using only his prosthetic arm, he flung the Director against the wall of his office. The Director's head hit the wall with an audible impact. He gave a bubbly cough, his eyes rolled up and he slumped heavily to the floor.

One of the security guards was coming round. He sat up, shook his head, gazed unbelievingly at the wreck of the Director's face, and stared uncomprehendingly at Conrad.

Conrad picked up his laser rifle and gave it to him. "Sorry I had to hit you and your friend . . . Ah, he is coming round, too. I think you had better arrest me."

17

"Yes, sir." The man stood up groggily. "What the hell is this all about, Commander? You have wrecked our careers. We have a right to know."

"Sorry again. Classified information . . . I don't think I have wrecked your careers. If there is an enquiry, trial or court-martial, I will testify that with complete disregard for personal safety, you subdued me and prevented me from inflicting more serious damage on that heap of blubber." He pointed at the unconscious Director.

The other guard pulled himself together and also stood up.

"Incidentally," said Conrad, "there is a certain Miss Angstrom next door. She can't have failed to hear the rumpus. Be good enough to let her know that you have subdued me. Also advise her that the Director is in immediate need of medical care and minor surgery. I don't like the look of his face."

Suddenly, both guards grinned. One of them said: "I never did like the look of his face, Commander, you are one hell of a man."

Phase Two

Bumf

MEMORANDUM

To: Secretary-General, United Nations.
From: Director, Extra-Solar Planets Evaluating and Normalising Department.
Subject: Commander James Conrad.
Para. 1. I have your acknowledgment of receipt of the account of Commander Conrad's extraordinary behaviour, which I dictated in hospital after undergoing surgery as a result of his unprovoked violence. I have learned with shock and amazement of the order for his subsequent release from detention in the maximum se-

18

curity block of Angmering Psychiatric Centre. My Deputy Director has informed me that this order originated in your office.

Para. 2. I realize, of course, that there is a delicate PR problem. Conrad, having proved two extra-solar planets for colonization, has achieved much notoriety. This, however, does not give him *carte blanche* for anti-social behaviour. The man is clearly a megalomaniac with homicidal tendencies. In the interests of justice, I would wish to see him discharged from ExPEND. If this is acceptable to you, I am prepared to waive my right to prefer criminal charges of intent to maim or kill. Alternatively, bearing in mind the public relations aspect, and anxious as I am to see that the image of ExPEND is not tarnished, if Conrad will resign the service immediately and submit voluntarily to psychiatric treatment, I will let the matter drop.

Para. 3. With respect, I must remind you that this man is not indispensable. The current ExPEND Recruitment and Training Programme has produced several men of command calibre. Of course, I would recommend that Captain Willard Sikorsky, late of U.N.S.S., nationality American, be used to fill—as it were—the psychological vacuum created by Conrad's dismissal/resignation. Sikorsky is an intelligent man with a distinguished record. I am sure that skilful exposure to the media would rapidly establish him as an international cult figure. In which case, I would be very happy to offer him command of the refurbished *Santa Maria* for the Argus project, the proving of the fifth planet of Alpha Lyrae (Vega).

MEMORANDUM

From: Secretary-General, United Nations.
To: Director ExPEND.
Subject: Commander James Conrad and allied matters.
Para. 1. Commander Conrad has submitted voluntarily to examination by a team of U.N. doctors and psychiatric specialists. Their report indicates that, though he is an aggressive man, self-opinionated and impatient of stupidity or weakness, he is not abnormal in any clinical sense. Indeed, as you know, these very qualities have yielded excellent professional results—as the study of

his conduct on the Kratos, Tantalus and Zelos projects shows.

Para. 2. With reference to the unfortunate assault upon your person: Conrad freely admits a personal motivation, but declines to explain it. He has, however, undergone polygraph interrogation, the results of which are classified.

Para. 3. With regret, I am loath to accept Conrad's dismissal from ExPEND. His record is good, his value to the entire operation is incalculable. I have had discreet talks with responsible people in the media; and I believe that further escalation of this international scandal can be avoided.

Para. 4. For political reasons, which I am sure you will appreciate, it is necessary to present the best credible aspect of this unfortunate affair. With your co-operation as Director of ExPEND, it should be possible—as far as the media are concerned—to minimize the significance of the incident. An appropriate interpretation would be along the following lines: Commander Conard has been subjected to immense pressures and strains during his successful proving projects. Therefore, in this context, the incident may be regarded as the result of a minor misunderstanding. If you would be so good as to indicate that you bear no personal animosity, that you have a great regard for his achievements, and that—after an extended leave—he will be re-assigned to command of the *Santa Maria* for the Argus project, I am confident that the matter will rapidly cease to be significant.

Para. 5. I hope you are now fully recovered.

Private and Personal Letter to Secretary-General, U.N., from Director ExPEND. (Not for the record.)

Dear Secretary-General,

Conrad made one hell of a mess of my face. There were multiple fractures of the jaw, and seven teeth were dislodged. If he will not resign the service immediately, I will do nothing to save him from the disgrace he richly deserves. The man is insufferable. Either he goes or I go. It is as simple as that.

Sincerely,
Charles T. Edwards
Director, ExPEND.

Private and Personal Letter to Director, ExPEND from
Secretary-General, U.N. (Not for the record.)

Dear Director,

I am sorry to learn of your intransigent attitude. I now expect to receive your letter of resignation as Director of ExPEND on any of the following grounds: mental exhaustion, ill health, domestic problems, a desire to emigrate to Mars or Luna.

My investigators have revealed that you have substantial financial interests in Self-Programming Robots Inc. No action is contemplated—at the moment.

Sincerely,
Roald Amundsen
Secretary-General, U.N.

Phase Three

What Kind of People Are You?

The small, white-haired man sitting at the desk looked up at Conrad and sighed. "What am I to do with you, Commander Conrad?"

Conrad, in best dress uniform with cap under arm, flanked by two U.N. guards, stood stiffly to attention. He had never met Roald Amundsen before. The man looked weighed down with the cares of office. Conrad was sorry to have added to his burdens.

"I really don't know, sir."

"Your attack upon the Director of ExPEND has created a great deal of trouble and brought much unwelcome publicity."

"I'm very sorry, sir."

Amundsen rewarded him with a thin smile. "Do you propose to put me in hospital if we should disagree?"

"No, sir."

"Then I may dismiss the guards without fear of suffering personal injury thereafter?"

"Yes, sir." There was just a hint of reproach in Conrad's voice. He had no quarrel with the Secretary-General.

Amundsen waved his hand in a dismissive gesture, and the two guards left the office, Conrad continued to stand to attention, eyes apparently gazing without focusing at some point about a metre above the Secretary-General's head.

"Commander, I have no military rank and this is not a court-martial. Please relax. Take a chair, and we will try to deal with this problem."

"Thank you, sir." Conrad sat down.

"You realize that, apart from any disciplinary action, the Director of ExPEND is entitled to bring a charge of criminal assault?"

"Yes, sir."

The Secretary-General smiled. "Fortunately, he won't. That—as our American hosts would say—has been taken care of."

Conrad was mildly surprised. "How can you be sure, sir?"

"You are very discreet, Commander. It was left to my investigators to discover the Director's interest in Self-programming Robots Inc. . . . No, the real problem is the question of your own future and the future of ExPEND . . . This affair has occupied the solar news media far too long. It has polarized certain political factions. There are still some influential statesmen who wish to see ExPEND and its operations discredited—despite the fact that two new worlds have already been gained for colonization. These people have short-term interests. They would still like to see the massive investment necessary for ExPEND operations rechannelled to Third World development areas."

"So my neck is on the block," said Conrad tranquilly, "and there are several candidates for wielding the axe."

"Precisely. But there are further complications. If you are dismissed, or if you resign your commission, the ExPEND operation will fall apart anyway. This is a high price to pay for injuring someone you dislike, is it not?"

"Sir," said Conrad, "some of *my* people died because of the Director's stupidity and greed. I regret that I have created problems for you. I do not regret smashing that bastard. May I go, now?"

"No, you may not!" Suddenly, the Secretary-General's voice was hard. "I repeat: by your action you have placed the entire operation of ExPEND in jeopardy. My office has been inundated with telegrams and petitions from all over the world . . . How the details of the incident were leaked, I do not know. An enquiry is being carried out."

Conrad shrugged. "Apart from answering questions asked by authorized U.N. personnel, sir, I have made no comment, public or private."

The Secretary-General smiled. "I know. You were probably not aware of it, but you have been under very close surveillance."

"I was aware of it," said Conrad drily. "Expendables have to have a talent for noticing little things. Otherwise, they are very soon dead."

"Which brings me to another small matter. Are you aware that a number of your colleagues are attempting blackmail on your behalf?"

Conrad raised an eyebrow, then scratched his silver patch nervously. "I am not aware of—or responsible for —any action taken by any of my colleagues, sir. Perhaps you would explain."

Roald Amundsen picked up a document from his desk. "Among the telegrams I have received is this one: *In the event that Commander James Conrad be dismissed or asked to resign his commission, the resignations of the following members of ExPEND become automatic. Signed: Kurt Kwango, Indira Smith, Hal Joseph Mencken, Jane Ustinov, Gunnar Norstedt, Mirlena Robinson, Tibor Maleter, Maeve O'Brien.*" The Secretary-General let out a sigh of exasperation. "What kind of people are you Expendables? Almost certainly some of those who have signed this telegram would immediately go back to prison to serve the rest of their sentences for crimes committed, if they were to carry out their threat. What kind of people are you?"

"Sir," retorted Conrad, "you have answered your own question. We are criminals, misfits, social outcasts. We are a fraternity of the damned. We are not beautiful people, and we would be disastrous on the cocktail circuits of Terra. But we have found new worlds for man to colonize. When this beat-up old planet can't take any more, when the resources of the solar system are exhausted, we will have ensured that mankind will survive. Some of us have shed our blood in the process, some of us have already died many light-years from Earth . . . Yes, we *are* the scum of the Earth, sir. We are not very nice to know, but we are proud of our work, we have a certain style, and we try to take care of our own . . . May I go now?"

"No you may not . . . Commander Conrad, the Director of ExPEND has tendered his resignation. I am offering you his post. Will you accept?"

Conrad registered surprise but did not hesitate. "No sir. I am not cut out to be chairborne. May I go now?"

"Damnation, yes!" said the Secretary-General. "It was the answer I expected. Now you leave me with another parcel of diplomatic problems. But, just for once, you will obey orders. You will take an extended leave on doctor's advice because of stress, then you will reassume command of the *Santa Maria*, get out into space and prove Argus. Meanwhile, I will try to clear up the mess."

Conrad stood up and saluted. "Thank you, sir."

"Don't thank me, Commander. Prove Argus for colonization."

"We will do our best."

Amundsen stood up and held out his hand. "Good luck, then . . . But when you return to Terra, Commander, if you have a grievance against the next Director, *please* talk to me first."

Conrad took the proffered hand. "Yes, sir." Then with a faint smile, he added: "Maybe the next one will benefit from the experiences of his predecessor."

He left the office of the Secretary-General. A chopper was waiting for him. Ten minutes later, he was clear of

New York. Fifty minutes later, he transferred to a scheduled flight strato-rocket bound for Europe.

Phase Four

Intermezzo

Conrad had what so far had proved to be an infallible method of losing himself when he really wanted to, or when he needed to rest. Normally, wherever he went on Earth the news of his arrival would reach the gentlemen of the media within minutes. Even if he wore civilian clothes and a discreet plastic patch instead of the silver eye-patch that instantly identified him to nine thousand million Terrans, his face was too well known for an incognito to be preserved for long. Already, he had become an international folk hero, a living legend. He had even tried false beards and dark glasses. They didn't work. The spaceman's gait and the voice that was familiar to billions soon blew his cover.

But, fortunately, he had friends on Earth. Loyal friends. Friends who could not be bought. Specifically, he had friends in the Royal Air Force. Also he had a retreat, a place where he could relax—if only briefly—and pretend for a while that he was just an ordinary human being. The gentlemen of the media knew that he had such a place. But they did not know where it was or how he got there. The going rate offered for hard information about Conrad's hideaway by Intervid, Trans-Solar News, Time-Newsweek, Comtel and other giants in the communications industry was around a hundred thousand solars. Enough to make anyone reasonably wealthy. But Conrad's friends were not the kind of people who would sell his right to privacy for a hundred thousand solars.

He always used the same hotel in London, so the media men were waiting for him. But he used that hotel because he had friends there, too.

He walked through the main doorway, facing a barrage of questions, still and vid cameras. News of his meeting with the Secretary-General had inevitably leaked and had reached London ahead of him.

"Commander, is it true that you slugged the Director of ExPEND because you hold him responsible for the Janus disaster?"

"Commander Conrad, will you confirm that you have now been offered control of ExPEND operation?"

"Sir, it has been reported that you are undergoing psychiatric treatment. Would you care to comment?"

"Is there any truth in the rumour, Commander, that you had an intimate relationship with Ruth Zonis?"

Once, Conrad would have lost his temper with the gentlemen of the media. Once, he did. But that was on Luna after his court-martial. A long time ago. Three planets ago. Now he was older and, possibly, wiser. He realized he would have to make some kind of statement.

"Gentlemen, the responsibility for the Janus disaster can only be determined by investigation. Some of the people who died on Janus were close friends and had worked with me, as you know. I greatly admired Ruth Zonis, but our relationship was at all times strictly professional. I am not undergoing psychiatric treatment. But I have been ordered to rest. I hope you will allow me to do just that. I have nothing more to say."

Eventually, he managed to get to his room. The hotel security guards cleared the corridor. Conrad took a shower, and had a meal sent up to him. He drank some whisky—only enough to relax him—then undressed and went to sleep, having asked to be awakened an hour before daybreak and having made one call to RAF Tangmere. His friends knew what to do. It was almost a routine operation.

While the vid men camped in the foyer, having posted their minions at all known exits, Conrad departed unobtrusively in a large laundry basket which was taken down to the basement and loaded with a number of other baskets into a hovertruck. Ten minutes later he stepped out of the basket and boarded an RAF chopper waiting in Hyde Park. Twenty-five minutes after that, he was in the weapons co-ordination seat of a Mach 4 interceptor strato-jet at Tangmere.

The pilot took off and lifted on an almost vertical course through the troposphere at more than two G, knowing that his passenger was no stranger to G stress. At an altitude of twenty thousand metres, the interceptor levelled and streaked north, its destination the Inner Sound of Raasay, off the northwest coast of Scotland.

Within five minutes, it was on a descent course from the stratosphere through the troposphere. The pilot knew exactly what he had to do. His orders were to bring the interceptor down to one thousand metres over the Inner Sound, about a kilometre from the mainland, at near stalling speed.

He did just that.

"Thanks for the buggy ride," said Conrad.

"My pleasure, Commander."

Conrad pressed the ejector-seat button, and was shot out into the clean cool air of a Scottish morning like a human cannon ball. The chute opened and he began to drift down towards the water.

The sea was remarkably calm. The morning was perfect. The sun was just lifting over the north-west highlands. There was Applecross. And there was a figure on the beach, waiting.

For a few moments, Conrad felt godlike. He was not sitting on an ejector seat with an automatically inflatable dinghy and emergency survival equipment stowed under him. He was sitting on a gently swaying throne between sky and earth. It was champagne.

He hit the water. His sealsuit didn't allow it to penetrate, but he fancied he could feel the delicious bracing coldness. He hit a button and released himself from the seat. The dinghy inflated. Conrad hauled himself aboard. He extended the telescopic paddles, fitted them in the row-locks and started rowing. The emergency pack had surfaced and was following the dinghy with a plaintive bleep-bleep. Conrad ignored it. The only life-support system he needed was standing on the beach.

It was a woman. It was called Indira Smith. Surgeon-Lieutenant Indira Smith. It had prosthetic legs, its hair was white, its skin was brown, and it was entirely beautiful.

Phase Five

Glad Tidings

It didn't worry Conrad that Indira had what they both jokingly called tin legs, just as it did not worry her that Conrad had a tin arm and wore a patch over his implanted infra-red eye.

Indira had once been a Surgeon-Lieutenant of the Terran Disaster Corps on the Amazonia rehabilitation project. Then about thirty so-called freedom fighters had liberated her body in the traditional way, while making the man she hoped to marry watch the proceedings. Afterwards, they gouged his eyes out and cut off her legs. The timely arrival of a U.N. chopper had saved her life. But it had been a photo-finish.

It was a long time ago. Three planets ago. Now she was Lieutenant Smith, veteran Expendable, a beautiful woman with white hair, brown skin and an indomitable spirit.

Actually, the prosthetic legs—like Conrad's arm—were miracles of engineering design. They were made of titanium and steel, powered by tiny atomic motors. They were bio-integrated machines covered in skin-tinted plastic that was barely distinguishable from living flesh. They would run tirelessly all day if she told them to, or enable her to leap five metres in the air or kick a hole in a concrete wall.

But when Conrad lay between them, caressing her body, finding peace and ecstasy at the same time, whispering things to Indira, the woman, that he would never say to Lieutenant Smith, the Expendable, tin legs didn't matter.

28

All that mattered was the delight of sex and love, the luxury of stolen time.

The almost derelict fishing village of Applecross provided an ideal retreat for Conrad. There were few people left. They had an intense loyalty to each other and a great admiration and respect for the man with the silver patch, the man who had proved new worlds for the colonization of mankind. They gave him what he desired most of all—privacy. Conrad had a small cottage in a little clearing in a forest, about a kilometre inland. When he was in residence—which was not often—they set up their own early warning system of visitors. Conrad knew better than to try to bribe or buy the loyalty of these highlanders for whom time seemed to have stood still. But he talked with them, drank with them, fished with them. He called them by their first names, and they called him by his.

He had just spent a precious morning in bed with Indira, when an old man, Diarmid MacDiarmid, knocked tentatively and discreetly on the door of the cottage. With some reluctance, Conrad detached himself from Indira. She was lying spread-eagled on the bed, eyes closed, a dew of sweat on her forehead, a faint smile of fulfilment on her lips.

Conrad threw some clothes on hastily. "Who's that?" he called.

"James, it's me, Diarmid. I didna wish to disturb ye, but there is one o' them noisy floatin' contrivances coming up the Inner Sound awful fast. I think ye ha' visitors."

"Thanks, Diarmid. I'll be out in a moment." He turned to Indira. "Who the devil can it be?"

"Who else but Kurt?" She opened her eyes indolently, tried to focus and failed. "He's the only one who knows about Applecross."

"Kwango!" exclaimed Conrad. "Damn that black bastard. Doesn't he know that Applecross is forbidden territory?"

Indira opened her eyes again. This time she managed to keep them open. "You talk as if you owned this place," she said gently. She managed to sit up. "You gave me one hell of a going over," she said complacently. "I hope

29

you remember it when you start playing the tough paranoid disciplinarian about twenty light-years away."

Conrad gazed at her compact and delicious breasts, allowing himself a brief mental action-replay. "I lock my memories away until I need them," he said. "And, anyway, this *is* my territory. And when you are here you are just my woman. After Kratos and Tantalus and Zelos, I'm entitled to a little luxury—when I can get it . . . Now make yourself decent, woman, while I go with Diarmid and see what the invasion is all about."

Indira stood up, naked, beautiful, and saluted insolently. "Sir, yes, Commander, sir. At the double. You are a hard man, James Conrad."

"And you know where I like to be hard," he said drily. "Now, jump to it, hussy. Playtime is over."

He went out of the cottage and joined Diarmid.

By the time they got to the beach, the hovercar was racing in from the sea, etching a smooth foam-flecked curve on the calm water. It came straight towards them, leaving the water and gliding over the wet white sand and shingle. It grounded about ten metres from them. The motors died. Kwango got out.

"Blast and damnation!" said Conrad. Something told him that Kwango's visit was hardly the result of a sudden whim.

"Is he no welcome?" asked Diarmid. "If not, bear in mind ye ha' friends who will be happy to return the black gentleman to the sea, whence he came."

Conrad grinned. He had a sudden mental vision of Kwango being tossed into the Inner Sound. Whatever the odds, there would be a few highlanders who would remember the encounter with awe. Kurt Kwango, half Nigerian, half German, was a formidable man.

"Thank you, Diarmid. It will not be necessary. This man is Kurt Kwango, also my friend."

"So!" The old man's eyes brightened. "It is the Kwango himself. I will leave you, James, since he will doubtless have that to say which is not for my ears. But you and your lady and maybe the Kwango will drink with us this night some good Scotch whisky. Also, there will be some of the old songs."

"I hope so, Diarmid. I greatly hope so."

"Well, then, I'll away." The old man bowed his head courteously to Kwango, and made his way back up the beach.

Kwango came up to Conrad. "Hell, Boss, I been trying to call you for hours. Has de little box gone bust?"

"I didn't bring my transceiver. I never do. You should know that. The moment I used it, some bastard would get a d/f fix. Then choppers full of vid men would start coming out of the sky, and that would be the end of Applecross—*my* Applecross." He gazed at Kwango coldly. "Incidentally, Kwango, this part of the Highlands is a prohibited area for black scum—except by invitation. I do not recall having issued an invitation."

Kwango grinned amicably. "I just knew dis little ole nigger could rely on de traditional hospitality of de white trash . . . Boss, you are in the shit; and yet again the faithful Kwango rides to save you." He rolled his eyes and let out a sigh. "And this is how you greet me. Sad, very sad. If I were not an idealist, I could lose faith in human nature."

"Cut the funnies." Conrad scratched his silver eyepatch irritably. "What brings you, Kurt?"

"You want the good news first or the bad?"

"The bad. And it better be bad enough to justify this intrusion."

"Score one, Boss. It is. When did you last see the U.N. Secretary-General?"

"Yesterday. He told me to take an extended sick leave, which I am now busy doing."

Kwango shrugged. "A lot can happen in twenty-four hours. Alas, Boss, you just lost an extended sick leave—under the care, I presume, of the admirable Surgeon-Lieutenant Smith. You are to get the hell off this planet fast. Further, you are to proceed with the proving of Argus at all possible speed."

"Who says so?"

"Roald Amundsen himself. When he couldn't contact

31

you, he contacted me. U.N. agents hauled me out of a bar in Johannesburg, with little courtesy, where I was just beginning to have a nice time, and got scars to prove it . . . Boss, you should not have bopped the Director of ExPEND. It has created problems."

"I know that," said Conrad impatiently. "But the bastard had it coming to him. Ruth, Chantana, Fidel, Yuri —you know the score."

Kwango nodded. "I know the score. But it has now been extended. Commander, fasten your seat belt. The Director is dead."

"Dead?" Suddenly, Conrad was appalled.

"Take it easy, Boss. You didn't hit him that hard. He took pills. It seems that when U.N. investigated, they found more than the business with Self-Programming Robots Inc. It's classified, so I don't know what it is. But I was told that he knew that U.N. knew. So he makes with the pills."

"Then why the devil should this affect me? And why should I have to disappear? Somebody has flipped. If I lift off from Terra now it will look as if I have something to hide."

Kwango sighed. "Boss, *I* know you can be very stupid, de good Lieutenant knows you can be very stupid, the Secretary-General knows you can be very stupid. You are the only one who doesn't know it . . . The scenario goes like this: several billion people know that you made some spectacular dis-improvements to the man's face and put him in hospital. Shortly afterwards, he dies. There is going to be a big howl for a public enquiry into cause of death, and a lot of dirt is going to be revealed. The investigation could take months, and you could be required to testify before two thousand three hundred and forty-seven different committees. And a lot of a shit could hit the fan. If you go quietly, maybe some of the dirt can be swept under the carpet. If you stick around, people who don't like you too much—and this may come as a shock, but there are such unenlightened people, chiefly bent politicos in banana republics—might think they could get a lot of status by discrediting you . . .

32

"For the time being, U.N. agents are sitting on the news of the Director's death. They have stuck his body in the cooler, and they are trying to work out a scenario in which he officially dies while you are *en route* for Argus. But they don't have too much time available. The media boys got influential friends."

"I see. Recommendations, Kurt?"

"That we jet to Kennedy pretty damn soon. I have alerted the rest of the team. They are on their way. A ground-to-orbit vessel is on the pad and waiting. If we don't waste too much time, we can get ourselves up into the *Santa Maria* and efficiently chilled within twenty-four hours. Next time we hit room temperature we are in orbit round Argus. And how do you like that?"

"I don't. But it seems like a good idea. Let's stroll back to the cottage and tell Indira—Lieutenant Smith—that the party is over . . . She is not going to like it . . . So, I've had the bad news. What's the good news?"

"I got a letter for you from Roald Amundsen, Boss. It confirms his personal order that we blast off for Argus soonest. He signed it personally, so you are now fireproof."

"Good. I may need that when or if we ever get back to Terra. Elephants are not the only mammals with long memories."

"I got more good news, Boss," said Kwango. "You just invited me to lunch."

"I wasn't aware of it," retorted Conrad. "My remaining time and privacy are precious."

"De good Lieutenant would approve," said Kwango.

"I doubt it. We don't have much food in the cottage."

"Boss, I got a thermally insulated hamper in the hover-car. It contains the following items: three chilled bottles of genuine French champagne—*Veuve Cliquot* '73, one half kilo of smoked Scotch salmon, one pot of Beluga caviar, a loaf of stone-ground English bread and some Danish butter, a cold roast free-range chicken, Dutch tomatoes and French radishes, Alpine strawberries and a jar of Swiss cream. Now you know why you just invited me to lunch."

Conrad grinned. "It's blackmail. O.K., let's get the hamper and take the glad tidings to Lieutenant Smith."

Phase Six

More Bumf

Data Sheet: Project 4 SM/C

Copies to: Secretary-General, U.N.
Deputy Director, ExPEND
Admiral of the Fleet, U.N. Space Service
Controller, Kennedy Space Port
Logistics Office, Department of Colonization

Project: The proving of Argus, 3rd planet of Vega (Alpha Lyrae), distance 26 light-years.

Résumé: Data obtained by robot probe's orbital survey of Vega Three is as follows:

1. Planet is E-type, possessing 87% E-mass. Atmosphere contains 77.01% nitrogen, 21.01% oxygen, 0.97% carbon dioxide plus traces of neon, helium, krypton, xenon, argon and radon. Biosphere organically rich. Normal carbon cycle functions.

2. Planetary surface covered 68% by ocean. Land masses consist of one major continent (temperate to subtropical E-norm), two minor continents, one possessing polar ice cap, and numerous small islands. Mountain ranges, lakes and rivers monitored on continents and some larger islands.

3. No signs of radio emission, abnormal radio-activity, industrial pollution. No indication of existence of cities, communications networks or other structures associated with presence and organization of intelligent life-forms. Magnetometric and televid surveys indicate probable ex-

istence of substantial mineral deposits including coal, petroleum, iron, copper, bauxite, etc.

4. Interim estimate of ultimate optimum colonization potential: approx 3,000,000,000.

*   *   *

Vessel assigned for projected proving operation: Santa Maria. This vessel is equipped with three propulsion systems. (1) Thermo-nuclear drive for interplantary operations. (2) Conventional rocket engines for orbital manoeuvre, lift-off and touch down. (3) Gravi-magnetic pulse generator and cosmometer for F.T.L. transit. Minor internal and external modifications have been made at the request of Commander James Conrad, ExPEND, as a result of his experience on previous operations (c.f. files Kratos, Tantalus).

*   *   *

Complement of *Santa Maria* re projected proving Planet Three Alpha Lyrae.

Conrad, James. Commander, Expendables, Team Four. Nationality, British. Ex-commander United Nations Space Service, formerly captain. Distinguished Space Service Cross and bar. Resigned from U.N.S.S. after being reduced to rank of commander as a result of court-martial. Court-martial findings: guilty as charged in willfully and repeatedly disobeying orders when permission to attempt rescue of crew of *S.S. Einstein* in decaying solar orbit was denied; not guilty of putting at risk his own vessel; guilty of causing deaths of three of his crew members and one engineer officer in attempted rescue. Conrad himself badly injured in this operation. Now has prosthetic right arm, and infra-red eye implanted in vacant right socket. Artificial eye normally covered by silver patch. Awarded Grand Cross of Gagarin for services rendered on Kratos.

Smith, Indira. Second-in-Command, Expendables, Team Four, Nationality, Indian. Ex-Surgeon-Lieutenant, Terran Disaster Corps. Resigned commission following torture and severe injuries inflicted by terrorists in Brazil.

Now has prosthetic legs. Awarded Distinguished Space Service Cross for services rendered on Kratos.

Kwango, Kurt. Ecologist, Expendables, Team Four. Nationality, Nigerian. Previously convicted criminal with history of violence. Behaviour since recruitment by ExPEND irreproachable. Granted free pardon for crimes committed. Awarded U.N. Gold Medallion for services rendered on Kratos and Polaris Star for services rendered on Tantalus.

Norstedt, Gunnar. Engineer, felon. Nationality, Swedish. Convicted by West German court for attempted political assassination. Released from prison under U.N. Mandate 31-B-9-72 and placed in custody of ExPEND for indefinite period.

O'Brien, Maeve. Chemist, felon. Nationality, Irish. Convicted by Irish court for armed robbery with violence. Released from prison under U.N. mandate 31-B-9-72 and placed in custody of ExPEND for indefinite period.

Maleter, Tibor. Geologist, weapons expert, felon. Nationality, Hungarian. Convicted by Soviet Court of political assassination. Found guilty but insane. Verdict challenged by three internationally eminent jurists. Subsequently released from Leningrad maximum security asylum under U.N. Mandate 31-B-9-72 and placed in custody of ExPEND for indefinite period. Note: independent psychiatric examination established Maleter's sanity within acceptable parameters.

Robinson, Mirlena. Biologist, felon. Nationality, American (black). Convicted by Chilean court of sabotage. Released from prison under U.N. Mandate 31-B-9-72 and placed in custody of ExPEND for indefinite period.

*   *   *

Special Equipment.

Robots, 6. Type: S.P.9. Robot S.P.9/1 has command circuitry which can override independent circuitry of others. Robots designated for convenience as: Matthew, Mark, Luke, John, Peter, Paul.

Helicopters, 1. Type: Multi-purpose T/N17a. Air-cooled/water-cooled. Maximum payload: one tonne. Sealed and shielded fuel system. Maximum range on primary fuel injection: 50,000 kilometres.

Hovercars, 1. Type: Variable lift, auxiliary jet, T/N5/8. Air-cooled/water-cooled. Maximum lift: three metres. Maximum payload: one tonne. Sealed and shielded fuel system. Maximum range on primary fuel injection: 75,000 kilometres.

Exo-skeletons, 7. Type: Superman 3. Dual power system: electro/hydraulic. Amplification factor 50. Maximum manipulative load: 5 tonnes. Sealed and shielded fuel systems. Maximum operability on primary fuel injection: 1–5 E-years.

Laser rifles, 15. Standard model U.N. 75, modified to reduce 10 centimetre plate of B.S.117 carbon steel at range of 5,000 metres.

Laser torches, 3. Standard model U.N. 75, modified to reduce all known metals at close range.

Anaesthetic guns, 7. Hand-gun type, 4: Magnum type, 3.

Suspended animation units, 7. Type S.A.5 dual system modules (self-regulating and/or star-ship regulated). Maximum operability 10–5 E-years.

Matter-receiver, 1. Type, sub-spatial U.R. Reception capacity, 500 kilogrammes in modular units at intervals of 6–45 minutes. Sealed and shielded systems. Maximum acceptance sequence, 200 units.

*   *   *

Recommendation: Go.

Decision approved by U.N./ExPEND/U.N.S.S. Evaluation Committee.

Phase Seven

The Last Supper

The Expendables came together at Kennedy Space Port. Conrad, Lieutenant Smith and Kwango were the first to arrive, having travelled together by strato-rocket to New

York and then by sub-strato jet down to Kennedy.

It was as Kwango had said. The ground-to-orbit vessel was on the pad, ready and waiting—a slender metal column three hundred metres high, capable of lifting a payload of one hundred and fifty tonnes. It would have to, because all the material for the Argus venture—Expendables, robots, equipment and supplies—was scheduled to be lifted to the two-hour orbit for rendezvous with the *Santa Maria* in one blast.

Maeve O'Brien was the next to arrive. She had taken a Trans-Terra strato from Tokyo where, after the intensive training course, she had been spending her precious leave. The first available Trans-Terra had been routed for Montreal. From there, she had jetted sub-strato direct to Kennedy.

She was a tall, slender, dark-haired woman with a pale but attractive face and expressive Celtic eyes. She was also a brilliant chemist and had been seriously considered for a Nobel Prize for her pioneer work on the chemistry of mammalian clone support systems. And she was also a political firebrand. When a small tribe in Central Africa was in danger of extinction because of continued drought —U.N. and the Disaster Corps being too busy with more urgent problems to do anything about—Maeve O'Brien organized a bullion raid on the Bank of Ireland. Enough gold was taken—exactly enough—to buy the necessary rain-making equipment. The raid was carried out with mathematical precision, and the African tribe got its rain-making gear and the services of a technical adviser. But, after inhaling anaesthetising gas which had been mysteriously polluted by a toxic agent, one Bank guard had a heart attack and died, and another suffered irreversible brain damage. On discovering this, Maeve O'Brien surrendered herself to the Irish police the very day she learned of her Nobel nomination. She had served two years of a long sentence when she was recruited by ExPEND.

Tibor Maleter got to Kennedy within minutes of Maeve O'Brien. He had been taking his leave in Hungary—mostly drinking with old friends and enjoying the attention of various highly attractive ladies who could thereafter make a double boast: that they had slept with an Expendable and also with the man who lasered the First Secretary of the Communist Party of the Soviet Union. Maleter could not deny that he had killed Comrade Bukharin since there were many reliable witnesses. Nor could he deny that he hated Bukharin's policy of suppressing the new liberal communism in the satellites while appearing to encourage it in the Soviet Union. What he did claim was that the assassination was carried out while he was under the influence of a compulsion drug. The defence request for immediate analysis of blood and urine samples had been denied. The trial was carried out with remarkable speed —one Russian, one Hungarian and one Indian psychiatrist having hastily pronounced him unfit to plead. There was an international outcry. Eventually, the Russians were glad to get rid of him to ExPEND. He had become a source of embarrassment.

Gunnar Norstedt came next to Kennedy. In contrast to Tibor Maleter, who was thin, nervous and wiry, Gunnar Norstedt was a typically big, amiable, extrovert Swede. Also, in contrast to Maleter, he had wanted to kill the West German chancellor and had failed. He had wanted to kill the chancellor because of certain ambiguous references made by Konrad Brandt to the achievement of one Adolf Hitler in the early twentieth century. Norstedt was drunk at the time. Too drunk to hold his laser pistol steady. He burned nine microphones, a large plaster cast of the German eagle, a cluster of balloons and a wisp of the luxuriant hair of Chancellor Brandt's wife before he was overpowered. The occasion was the Oktoberfest in Munich. Everybody laughed—except Frau Brandt.

The last to arrive was Mirlena Robinson. Black, American, entirely beautiful. High, firm breasts; rounded hips; and a way of walking that made men catch their breath. Working with a team of U.N. argricultural advisers in Chile, she had made the mistake of becoming energetically involved in the tortuous maze of Chilean politics. She joined a small group dedicated to overthrowing the corrupt and monolithic regime. The group was part of a network of similar groups, each with a special task to be carried out when the time was ripe for revolution. Mirlena's group had been assigned to knock out the capital's telephone system. Unfortunately, the group had already been infiltrated by a government spy. Unlike her comrades, who were summarily executed, Mirlena, being a U.S. citizen, and a beautiful woman, received preferential treatment. When the secret police had finished with her, she was given excellent hospital care, intensive sedation, a fast trial and a long sentence. Fortunately, as a result of the sedation, she could not remember very clearly what had happened. After several months, the long arm of American diplomacy extracted her from an unhealthy and overcrowded prison as a volunteer Expendable.

Conrad was familiar with the dossiers of all his new recruits. On the whole, he preferred political offenders to common criminals. They were, perhaps, harder to handle; but, if they believed in something, they would go ahead regardless of cost. That was the quality he needed.

When they had all assembled, he took them to a small V.I.P. dining-room. "Times have changed," he said. "Before the first team lifted off for Kratos, we were starved for twelve hours, made to empty our bowels and sweat all the surplus fluid out of our bodies in the sauna. Then, while we were dwelling on that happy experience, the medics pumped sub-thermal shock injections into us, and stripped us down for the cooler." He glanced at Kwango and smiled faintly. "Our resident genius here tried to box clever. He ducked the sub-thermal shock needles and woke up dead in orbit round Kratos. Lieutenant Smith made history with the first zero G heart-transplant . . . However, since then progress has been made in the area of sub-thermal shock treatment. The medics now magnanimously allow us a last supper before we get chilled. Also, no sauna and no forced evacuation. That is what I call a really civilized attitude. But we are rationed to eight ounces of lean steak each—no side dishes—and two glasses of red wine, which, happily, has to be not less than fourteen degrees proof spirit. I have taken the liberty of ordering the steaks—I'm told they have to be very well done, not rare—and two litres of *Châteauneuf du Pape*

40

'73. Please take your seats. Two hours from now, we get the needles. Three hours from now we hit the ice."

The dining table was ready, the robo-waiters were ready, the steaks were ready and the wine was uncorked.

"Boss, I did not duck the sub-thermal treatment," said Kwango, casually taking the chair next to Mirlena.

"Kurt, when we got back to Terra, I checked the records. A certain Leopold Blenkinsop signed that he had given you the shots. There never was any Leopold Blenkinsop in the medic group."

Kwango shrugged. "You know what bureaucracy is like, Boss. Most of the people at Kennedy don't know what the others are doing."

Conrad sighed. "Kwango, this one you lost. I asked for calligraphic analysis of the signature. Need I say more?"

"No, Commander. You already said too much . . . This wine has an amusing presumption, don't you think?" Kwango put down his glass and smacked his lips noisily.

"It matches the man who drinks it," retorted Conrad.

"Commander," said Mirlena, "why do we have to go into suspended animation before we are in the *Santa Maria*? I don't much like the idea of being shot upstairs like a frozen Frankfurter."

"I don't care for it too much myself," admitted Conrad. "There are two basic reasons. One: these dirtside medics don't like to operate suspended animation procedure in zero G if they can avoid it—though I, personally, think it's more because they are not too keen on enduring lift-off stress themselves. The other reason is simply money. The Administration likes to save a few solars wherever it can. The cost of lifting two or three tonnes of medics and their gear into orbit is probably enough to pay for about ten expense-account lunches . . . Now, let's enjoy the steak. None of your soya-meat, this. It's honest Scotch steak. Eat it with reverence."

They did.

Presently, Tibor Maleter said: "Why has our leave been shortened, sir? I thought we would have ten more days before reporting for duty."

Conrad sipped the *Châteauneuf du Pape* appreciatively. "Sorry, Tibor. I'm afraid it is partly my fault. When I lost my temper with the Director, there were some unforeseeable repercussions. As a result, the Secretary-General of U.N. wants me out of the solar system fast."

"You didn't hit that man hard enough," said Maeve O'Brien fiercely. "You only put him in hospital."

Conrad scratched his silver eye-patch nervously. "It was a private matter, Maeve. What do you know about it?"

She tossed her dark hair and laughed. "Only what several billion other people know—that you considered him to be directly responsible for the Janus disaster."

"I hit him hard enough," said Conrad drily. "He's dead. That is classified information, so you will mention it to no one dirtside. Now you know why we have to lift off before he becomes officially dead."

Gunnar Norstedt raised his glass. "By damn, Commander, you are one hell of a fellow . . . Ladies and gentlemen, I give you a toast: the health of Commander James Conrad, who——"

"Belay that!" snapped Conrad. "I didn't kill him. He killed himself. We are—all of us—the dregs of society, Norstedt. We are expendable. Apart from Lieutenant Smith, we have all broken the rules—one way or another. But no one under my command will ever rejoice in the death of another human being. That is an order . . . If you want to drink a toast, Gunnar, I'll give you one that is worth drinking to." Conrad lifted his own glass. "To the proving of Argus—one more for stupid old *homo sap!*"

Norstedt smiled. "If such is your pleasure, Commander. But you are still one hell of a fellow . . . To the proving of Argus, then."

Seven glasses were raised.

Lieutenant Smith whispered very softly so that no one else would hear: "James Conrad, I love you."

"Lieutenant," said Conrad, also very softly, "as of now, you are on duty. Remember that."

"Yes, Commander. I will remember that. Other things also."

Kwango spoke. "Boss, we had it rough on Kratos, you also got yourself smashed up on Tantalus, and Zelos was a kind of Mexican stand-off . . . This time, I think we are going to be lucky. Something tells me that Argus is going to be a nice relaxing holiday. I have gone over the data supplied by the robot probe, and it looks as if Argus could be a Garden of Eden."

Conrad helped himself to some more wine. "Kurt, you are brilliant, as always."

"Thanks, Boss."

"And, as always, you are very stupid . . . All right, everyone. The party's over. Let us prepare to be chilled."

Phase Eight

Do You Know Who You Are?

Conrad lay naked on the intensive care bench in the *Santa Maria*'s resuscitation chamber. Earth was now twenty-six light-years away, and the star-ship was in stable orbit round Argus, at an altitude of one thousand kilometres. But Commander James Conrad neither knew nor cared, being neither alive nor dead but a little of both.

A robot bent over his body. It had the word Matthew painted on its chest plate and its back plate. Matthew wore thermal gloves so that its steel fingers would not harm the pale, vulnerable flesh and so that radiant heat could be applied where it was most needed.

Conrad's body looked as if it was drenched with sweat; but this was really a heavy dew, the coldness of the flesh condensing water vapour out of the warm air. Patiently, Matthew sponged the dew away, simultaneously monitoring the minute changes of body temperature, the weak and still sporadic heart-beat, the barely detectable surges of blood pressure.

On the nav deck, the robot Mark was at the command console, monitoring the condition of the ship's electronic, mechanical, life-support and propulsion systems as carefully as Matthew watched over the condition of its commander. In the engine-room—or reaction control complex, as it was officially described—Luke was going through the intricate procedure of shutting down the gravi-magnetic pulse generator that had enabled the *Santa Maria* to create its own modified black hole in the space-time continuum and leap (dive under?) all the light-years that separated Sol from Vega. John was adjusting the recycling unit in anticipation of the fact that presently seven human beings would be using oxygen, exhaling carbon dioxide, ingesting liquid and food, urinating and excreting. The other two robots, Peter and Paul, were readying food and equipment in anticipation of the requirements of those inefficient bio-machines designated as human beings. All five robots fed their data back to Matthew, who absorbed and stored it even as he restored the life-function to Conrad.

Gentle, rhythmic pressure on the chest had now triggered the breathing cycle. The heart was gaining strength, the pulse was steadying, blood pressure was approaching normal. Conrad groaned. His bio-arm twitched, so did his legs. Suddenly, he opened his eyes and groaned once more. Then he closed them again.

Matthew placed a mask over his nose and mouth. Oxygen-enriched air, synchronized with the breathing cycle, was pumped into the lungs.

Conrad opened his eyes again. This time he kept them open, but cried out in anguish. Matthew knew what was happening. The vision analysis centres of the brain were receiving contradictory signals. Matthew took the silver patch and placed it over the right eye.

Conrad took a deep breath and relaxed. He managed to smile. Then he said weakly: "Here we go again, Matthew."

"Sir, do you require orientation?"

44

There was a pause. Then Conrad said: "No, I don't think so. Every time I get chilled, my tolerance seems to increase . . . Interesting . . . The law of diminishing returns seems also to apply to the temporary amnesia we are supposed to get coming out of S.A. *Very* interesting."

"Sir," said Matthew patiently, "do you know who you are?"

Conrad said: "I know I am bloody cold."

"That is understood, sir. Sub-thermal trauma induces ——"

"Belay that crap. Get me a large brandy."

"Sir, query term: belay that crap."

"Cancel statement," snapped Conrad. "Get me the brandy."

"Sir, it is not advisable to consume brandy at this stage. Do you know who you are?"

Conrad sat up, shivering, bad-tempered. "I am James Conrad, Commander, Expendables, Team Four. Unless somebody or something has fucked it all up, the *Santa Maria* is now in orbit round the planet designated as Argus. Now get that brandy, and make it a large one, you stupid bastard."

Conrad passed a hand over his forehead, and felt the still cold dew. "Cancel statement, Matthew. I'm sorry."

Matthew permitted himself a touch of robotic humour. "It is not necessary to express regret, sir. While you were identifying yourself, Paul was re-routed to extract one bulb of liquid designated as Hennessy XO from Number One hold. He will be here in one point two five minutes, plus or minus 5 per cent."

Despite the pain and the cold in his limbs, Conrad grinned. "Matthew, old friend, what would I do without you?"

Again that apparent flash of robotic humour. "It is probable, sir, that you would have remained in suspended animation for an indefinite period, sir."

Conrad shook his head wonderingly. No S.P.9 robot— not even an S.P.9/1—could be programmed for humour or irony . . . That double use of "sir", for example, was not robotese . . . It required a bisociative matrix to parallel the logic circuits. And yet . . . Perhaps the hidden hand of Kwango . . . But, no. The black genius was master of many skills, but not of robotics.

Bang on schedule, Paul brought the brandy. Expertly, Conrad squeezed the bulb and gave himself a large shot. He coughed appreciatively, felt the wonderful warmth trickle down inside him, and repeated the process. His limbs stopped hurting and began to tingle almost pleasantly. He didn't care a damn about the dew that dripped from his still cold forehead and into his eyes.

"If you are now ready, Commander Conrad, I will conclude the treatment and restore your life-function to normal. Estimated processing time eleven point five minutes."

Surely there could not be a note of sarcasm in that flat metallic voice? Conrad dismissed the notion and turned to matters practical. Docilely, he lay back on the intensive care bench while Matthew, with consummate skill, used the thermal gloves to ease away the musclar aches and pains that were a result of suspended animation.

Presently, the treatment ended. Presently, Conrad was towelled down and then put on his clothes. He felt desperately hungry. One always did after coming out of S.A.

Matthew knew that also. "Sir, do you now wish to order a meal? Milk, lean meat and red wine are recommended at this stage."

Perversely, Conrad said: "No, Matthew, I do not want a meal now. I am going to the nav deck. Have some coffee sent to me. You know how I like it. And pull Lieutenant Smith and Mr. Kwango out of S.A. with all possible speed. I will wait until they are viable before I eat."

"Decisions noted, sir. Execution proceeds. Query, sir: in what order do you wish the other members of the team to be resuscitated?"

Conrad scratched his eye-patch irritably. "I have not yet decided. Concentrate on Smith and Kwango. I will schedule the others later."

"Decision noted. Execution proceeds."

Conrad knew very well why, despite his intense hunger, he had declined to eat. He wanted to wait until Indira and

Kurt could take a meal with him. It was fast becoming a tradition. He remembered Tantalus and Zelos. It was good to have some time alone with close and trusted friends (damnit! was Indira only a friend—a sexual friend?) before the action started. Belay that thought . . .

On the nav deck, Mark reported. "All systems normal, sir. The vessel is in stable orbit at one thousand kilometres. Probe data confirmed. Preliminary survey of planetary surface indicates no radio emission, no atmospheric pollution, no industrialization, no significant radioactivity, no artificial structures, no sign of organization and/or constructions by intelligent life-forms as defined in Ex-PEND Manual 73/5."

"So Argus is going to be a piece of cake," observed Conrad caustically.

"Query, sir," said Mark. "Please define the term a piece of cake."

"Cancel statement."

"Decision noted. Execution proceeds."

Paul brought a bulb of coffee. It was hot, black and sweet—just as Conrad liked it. He took a couple of squirts, then walked carefully over the bond-fuzz towards the observation panel. You had to plant each foot very firmly on the carpet so that the hooked bristles would grip the soles of your boots. Conrad, being a veteran spaceman, made the motions automatically. So did the robots in their special zero G slippers. But the other members of the team, Conrad knew from sad experience, would come adrift many times and float helplessly or collect a few bumps and bruises before they mastered the art. Even the agile Kwango and Lieutenant Smith, who had ample experience of zero G on the three previous missions, would take off once or twice before they regained their space legs.

That thought reminded him to call Matthew on the intercom. "You are working on Lieutenant Smith?"

"Yes, Commander."

"How goes it?"

"I have commenced the second phase of thermal heart massage. Temperature is still several degrees below in-

47

dependent life-support. I record intermittent heart response. Breathing cycle still unactivated. Condition normal for this stage. Do you wish me to report when viability is established?"

"Yes. How long will that be?"

"Decision noted. Estimated time factor now thirty-five minutes S.E.T. plus or minus 5 per cent."

"Thank you."

Conrad had a sudden vivid mental picture of that small, beautiful, naked body strapped to the intensive care bench. Matthew's thermal glove would be massaging gently round the firm brown breasts in a grotesque parody of love play. Conrad had seen it once and he didn't want to see it again. With an effort, he cancelled the image. He knew his revulsion was irrational. A robot could take no pleasure from handling a naked woman. But the very thought offended some basic taboo . . .

To distract himself, Conrad pressed the stud that rolled back the screen covering the observation panel.

Phase Nine

The First Breakfast

The *Santa Maria* was passing over the night side of Argus. Five hundred thousand kilometres away, there was a full moon—almost the size of Earth's moon. It transmuted the bright gold Vegan sunlight into soft silver and reflected it down to Argus, bathing the planet in a silvery glow.

Most of the major continent was dimly visible, as were vast reaches of ocean. The continent was huge and, in shape, looked somewhat as if South America and Africa had been slotted together—as geologists said was the case in Terra's distant past.

"So we'll call it Amafrica," said Conrad aloud.

"Query, sir," said Mark. "Please define relevance of statement."

Conrad had forgotten that he was not alone. "Cancel statement," he said without taking his gaze from the observation panel. "I was talking to myself."

He thought of asking the robot to set up the the manual telescope, then decided against it. Visibility conditions were not good enough even for low magnification survey. There would be plenty of time to select a touch-down area when everyone was out of S.A.

Conrad sighed. Amafrica looked peaceful enough as it rolled slowly below the *Santa Maria*. But, despite Kwango's optimism, a sixth sense—and bitter experience—warned Conrad that Argus would have its own special brand of surprises.

He did not for one moment believe that the data supplied by the robot probe had any real relevance to surface conditions. A robot probe had reported that Kratos was O.K. for proving. But it had not given any indication of the presence of the monstrous deathworms that dominated the ecology. A robot probe had given the go-ahead for Tantalus, failing to register the deadly power of the rings or the existence of those grotesque robot guardians. And a robot probe had failed to notice the presence of a small but complex *human* society on Zelos.

The hell with probe data! And the hell with Kwango's stupid optimism! Argus was going to be tough. Conrad could feel it in his bones.

Matthew reported. "Lieutenant Smith is viable, sir. Responses excellent, recall complete."

"Thank you. Get her dressed, then send her—no, ask her—to join me on the nav deck."

"Decision noted. Execution proceeds."

"Now get Kwango up to room temperature with all possible speed."

"Query, sir. Is the situation designated as an emergency?"

"No, it is not. Just bring that black bastard out fast. I'm hungry."

"Query, sir. Do you wish to eat Mr. Kwango?"

Conrad restrained an impulse to blast the robot verbally. It wouldn't do any good. Matthew would retreat into robotese, and Conrad would end up cancelling half a dozen statements. But the veiled humour was beginning to pall.

"No, Matthew, I do not wish to eat Mr. Kwango. I wish to eat *with* him. Do you understand?"

"Thank you, sir, for the clarification."

Conrad was convinced he heard a robotic chuckle. But that was impossible.

Presently, Lieutenant Smith joined him.

"Well, James?"

"Well, Indira? How do you feel?"

"Bloody ravenous. But all systems go."

"I'll order some coffee for you."

"Have *you* eaten?"

"No."

"Why don't we eat together, then?"

"Because I am waiting for Matthew to bring out that stupid black bastard," Conrad said evasively.

Indira kissed him. "James Conrad, I love you. You have a great affection for Kurt."

Conrad tried to ignore the kiss and tried to ignore both statements.

"Lieutenant," he said, "I need that clever ego-maniac to do some thinking. That's what he's paid for."

"Nonsense. You may look like a space pirate, but you are just a sentimental teddy bear, heavily disguised."

"Lieutenant," said Conrad, trying to sound tough and still failing, "I would remind you that as of now you are on duty."

"Does kissing constitute assaulting a superior officer?"

"It does."

She kissed him again. "Then you can log me for mutiny. But if you don't tell, I'm sure Mark won't."

"Query, Lieutenant," said Mark. "Tell what to whom?"

"Cancel statement," said Conrad. "Get more coffee, Mark. We're going to need it."

He smiled and took Indira's hand. "I know. These times are precious, because you and I and Kurt have stacked up a few spectaculars between us. But when the rest come

50

out, you are just Lieutenant Smith, one more Expendable, and I am the bloody autocrat who gets the show on the road. Understood?"

"Understood, Commander."

"Then while we are waiting for wonder boy, I'll show you what can be seen of Argus."

"You think it's going to be rough, don't you?"

Conrad gave a grim smile. "When has it not been? If Argus turns out to be easy I'll buy you an entire Paris collection and Kurt all the booze he can drink in a year."

*　　*　　*

The *Santa Maria* had passed over dayside and over nightside once more by the time Kurt Kwango came up to the nav deck.

"Greetings, Massa Boss," he said cheerily. "Dis pore nigger is ready once more to work himself to de bone on de old plantation."

"Cut the Uncle Tom crap," said Conrad severely. "I'm too hungry to wear it. Come and take a look at this old plantation. You can't see too much at the moment, but at least you can see the shape of Continent A. Interesting, isn't it?"

Kwango registered the oddly familiar shape almost instantly. "Boss, it's one hell of a coincidence. As if South America and Africa were cellotaped together, like the eggheads claim they once were on Terra. This suggests the basis for an interesting little theory on separation geology."

"Don't get clever so early, Kurt. It disturbs me. Anyway, in view of the similarity of shape I have designated Continent A as——"

"Amafrica," said Kwango.

"Must you always do that?" demanded Conrad coldly. "It's a very irritating habit. I do not like being anticipated —ever."

Kwango shrugged. "Sorry, Boss. It's the trauma of coming out of S.A. My mind is not too clear." He gave Lieutenant Smith a conspiratorial grin. "I'll calm down pretty soon . . . Did somebody say something about being

51

hungry? I second that motion."

Indira said: "Kurt, this fearsome one-eyed monster is as soft as a ripe banana. He hasn't eaten anything himself because he was waiting for us to come out of S.A. How do you like that?"

"I think maybe I am going to cry," said Kwango. "But I'm too hungry. Seems like only last night we ate steaks and drank red wine together, but it feels like it was——"

"Twenty-six light-years ago," said Conrad. He smiled. "Let's have the action replay. Only this time we can allow ourselves more steak, more wine, side dishes, cheese, biscuits, coffee and brandy. I'll call Matthew to programme it ten from now."

"Just the three of us," said Indira. "The man speaks poetry."

"Play it, Sam," said Kwango, rolling his eyes. "Play it again."

"What the devil does that mean?" asked Conrad.

"Humphrey Bogart, *Casablanca*."

"Who is Humphrey Bogart and what is the connection with Casablanca?"

"Boss," said Kwango, "don't take this as personal, but I have always known you were illiterate, in a manner of speaking. Next, you'll be asking who is Wilhelm von Shakespeare. No matter, the Lieutenant and I both love you and will take care of you in your dotage. Just lead us to de food, Boss. All is forgiven."

Conrad scratched his silver eye-patch. "Cool it, Kwango. You are getting a little too clever a little too soon."

Again Kwango shrugged. "The story of my life, Boss."

*　　　*　　　*

It was good to be taking a meal once more in the saloon of the *Santa Maria*, reflected Conrad. And the meal, though similar, by established tradition, to the last one taken on Earth, was considerably better, And the company was more select.

Maybe that was a bit unfair to the four still in the cooler. They had all distinguished themselves in the rigorous training programme. But, no matter how good they were, none of them had the kind of history that made Lieutenant Smith and Kwango special people.

Conrad was aware of his own limitations. He knew that when the going got rough he sometimes developed a kind of kamikaze syndrome. And he knew also that, when it happened, Kurt and Indira would somehow pick up the pieces and stitch Humpty-Dumpty together again. It had happened on Kratos, it had happened on Tantalus and, dammit, it had also happened on Zelos.

Kwango sipped his brandy appreciatively. He looked at Conrad and seemed to be reading his thoughts. "Boss, do us both a big favour. Don't get smashed up this time. It is very wearing on the nerves. Also it is counter-productive. You have a positive talent for making the shit hit the fan. Then I have to haul you out of the crap, and the good Lieutenant has to lose beauty sleep setting various bones and embroidering various parts of your person. Break the run. Please take it easy, this time. Argus looks like a nice place. If we choose the right spot for touchdown, maybe we can put in some sunbathing." He grinned. "I'd like to get a tan, even if nobody notices."

"So Argus looks like a nice place," retorted Conrad. "Kratos looked like a nice place, too! We're taking no chances, Kurt. Not now. Not ever . . . During the next three days, there's a lot of work to be done. When the others are out of the cooler, Lieutenant Smith will check us over and we'll get the S.A. out of our muscles. And you, Kurt, will use every instrument we have to make a survey of Amafrica. Also, you will use what you have between your ears to give me more data than that bloody robot probe did. Furthermore, I want a high-resolution contour map with major mountain ranges, plains, lakes, rivers, large areas of grassland, forest, desert, jungle delineated clearly. I want to know high probability areas for fossil fuel deposits, and I want recommendations for a variety of possible touchdown points, bearing in mind that we don't want to waste any time intensively exploring an area that cannot be colonized. Any questions?"

"Yes, Boss." Kwango injected a little sarcasm into his

voice. "When I have disposed of the trifling items you listed, I am wondering just what I am going to do with all my spare time."

Conrad registered the sarcasm. "I'm glad you mentioned that. I hereby appoint you Briefing Officer. When our four friends get defrosted, you will fill them in on our past experiences and on anticipated problems *re* Argus. Also you will familiarize them with touch-down procedure and primary exploration routine."

Indira finished her brandy and smiled. "Kurt, when will you ever learn? Even I can pinpoint the moment when Dr. Jekyll is about to turn into Mr. Hyde."

Conrad turned on her. "Lieutenant Smith, spare me the funnies. I want the others operational within six hours. If you and Matthew take them out of the cooler two at a time and operate resuscitation procedures simultaneously, it can be done. After that, I want E.C.G. and E.E.G. analysis on all of us. After that, you can support Kwango in the briefing sessions and supervise the work-out programme to get us into optimum physical performance in minimum time. O.K. Lieutenant?"

"O.K., Commander."

Kwango tried again, "Boss, while all this high-speed activity is going on, what, exactly, will *you* be doing?"

"*The Times* Crossword Puzzle," snapped Conrad. "But when I have finished that, I shall see to the safety of the vessel and the efficiency or otherwise of its complement. Then I will schedule the priorities for unshipping cargo. Then I will inspect the propulsion systems and the navigation equipment. Then, I hope, I will have the very great pleasure of considering Lieutenant Smith's report on the condition of the team. And after that, the privilege of going through the data you will presently supply . . . Don't worry, Kwango. We are all going to lead a rich full life. Any more questions?"

Kwango shook his head. "No, Boss. I don't want to get in any deeper."

Conrad smiled. "It was a pleasantly intimate breakfast, wasn't it?"

"James," said Indira, "you are a monster."

"I know. As of now, we are at action stations. You both have your orders. Get moving."

Lieutenant Smith and Kurt Kwango exchanged glances which seemed to say: Here we go again.

Stage Two

The Venom

Phase One

Maybe This Is the Garden of Eden

The rockets whined into silence. The *Santa Maria*'s landing torus rested firmly on smooth ground. Conrad had chosen the touch-down point well. Within a radius of one hundred kilometres there was a considerable variety of terrain.

Conrad was not the first to unstrap himself and get out of his contour-berth. He never was. He lay back, letting his muscles adjust to the G-stress which, though a little less than that of Earth, would present problems to the unwary for a while.

Gunnar Norstedt, the big, amiable Swede was the first up. And the first down. Weighing one hundred and two kilos E-grav, he went down with a thud.

"By damn!" he said comically.

Conrad grinned. "Now you know. Our muscles have not yet recovered from S.A. and zero G. For an hour or two, you will need to think carefully about walking and even more carefully about lifting. Do everything slowly. I don't want any broken bones before we go dirtside."

In a leisurely and cautious fashion, he unstrapped and stood up. He didn't attempt to walk at first. He flexed his muscles for a couple of minutes. Then, while the others were unstrapping, he checked various instruments on the command console. The ship's attitude was less than two degrees from vertical, and the torus-linked pressure meters indicated that the vessel had touched down on moderately hard ground, so there seemed to be little danger of the *Santa Maria* listing. All in all, it looked like a textbook landing.

"Shall I roll back the screen, Commander?" asked Kwango. "I'd like to take a look through the observation panel and see what is growing in the garden."

"In a minute, Kurt. General orders first. Ladies and gentlemen, now that we have arrived, our first task is to become operational—which means, as I said, that we have to be able to carry out our duties under Argus G without falling about. It won't take long. While this is going on, two of the robots will proceed through the air-lock and go dirtside. They know the drill—or, rather, Matthew knows the drill and will programme them. Their first task will be to check on the external condition of the vessel, which, according to instrumentation, is pretty good. Then they will set up four vid cameras and hook them into the command screens here on the nav deck. The vids are semi-rotating and will cover all approaches to the *Santa Maria*. Assuming no problems, the robots will then collect air, soil and vegetation samples and dump them in the air-lock . . . These ought to keep you, Maeve, and you, Mirlena, gainfully occupied in the lab. Again, assuming no problems, the robots will then set up a defence perimeter of electrified chain-wire. Then, if all goes well, us poor humans can go dirtside to smell the flowers. As you are aware, it is early morning, local time. We have quite a long day ahead of us and much can be accomplished. The Argus day is twenty-two hours, nineteen minutes, seven seconds Standard Earth Time. We will adjust our personal electrochrons to transform this into a twenty-four hour cycle. But the ship's chronometers will maintain S.E.T. I do not anticipate adjustment problems."

"Commander," said Tibor Maleter, "are you not being over-cautious? According to the data supplied by the robot probe—this data being confirmed by Mr. Kwango's orbital investigations—Argus is an almost perfect E-type planet. Surely it is a waste of time to re-check data that has already been double verified?"

Conrad scratched his silver eye-patch irritably. "Perhaps, Tibor, perhaps. But humour me. Before I became an Expendable, I was not religious. Now I am. I am a devout coward. Neither the robot probes nor the genius of Mr. Kwango informed me of the existence of the death-worms of Kratos, the bio-robots of Tantalus, or the people of Zelos. These came as enchanting surprises. Maybe I am getting old, but I don't fancy having too many more surprises. So I intend to treat Argus as hostile until otherwise proved. Understood?"

"Understood, Commander."

"O.K., Kurt. Roll back the screen. Let us take a look at this green and pleasant land."

At first glance, Argus looked as if it might justify Kwango's optimism. The *Santa Maria* had touched down on a large plain which appeared to be covered with a fairly short grass and a few shrubs. About twenty kilometres to the planetary north, there was a range of mountain—some of the higher ones apparently snow-capped. To east and west, the plain stretched into the hazy distance; but though it could not be seen, Conrad knew that a river came down in the west from the mountains, feeding a large lake around which there was a variety of vegetation. To the south there was woodland eventually becoming forest which, much farther south, became dense jungle.

Maeve O'Brien said: "It looks as if we have touched down in a very pleasant part of Amafrica. But I'm disappointed. I was hoping to see some animal life."

Kwango laughed. "Lady, when this tin bird fell out of the sky with rockets roaring and scattering sonic booms over half the continent, any life-form with a central nervous system would instantly shit itself then run for cover or dig a hole and dive in, according to whim, basic programming and capability. Fear not, the animal life, of which there is plenty, will presently be stupid enough to return. Then, doubtless, the good Commander will insist on us having Argus steak for dinner."

Matthew reported over the intercom from the engine-room. "The vessel is firmly grounded, Commander. Telemetry also indicates bedrock to be sound in immediate vicinity. Permission requested to close down propulsion systems."

"Permission granted. I will come down myself shortly to check fail-safe procedure."

"Decision noted. Close down proceeding. Peter and Paul have now assembled required equipment in the air-lock.

Permission requested to activate standard touch-down programme."

"Permission granted. I want the vids hooked to command screens ten from now."

"Decision noted. Execution proceeds."

Conrad turned to the Expendables. "Well, then. It appears that we have an almost perfect touch-down and the countryside looks fine. Ace, king, queen, jack. I don't like it."

"Maybe Mr. Kwango *is* right," said Mirlena Robinson. "Maybe Argus is the planet where things will be O.K."

"Black is not only beautiful," said Kwango, gazing at Mirlena's superb figure approvingly, "it is also highly intelligent."

Conrad ignored him. "I hope you are right, Mirlena. On the three previous missions, I had to accept casualties. I'd like very much if we all came out of this mission in one piece . . . Now, to work . . ."

"Lieutenant Smith, you will remain on the nav deck and monitor the screens until relieved. Tape anything that looks interesting. I'll take over when I have attended to various other matters."

"Ay, ay, sir."

"Kwango, you will correlate vicinity data as received. If you find anything nasty, call me immediately. Otherwise, give me a précis I can read before lunch."

"Yes, Boss."

"Robinson and O'Brien, you will presently be getting air, soil and vegetation samples. First, I want to know if we can safely go outside without life-support packs. If the air contains any micro-organisms that you don't know about or that are not nice, buzz Kwango immediately. Second, I want comparisons between organic structures in soil and vegetation and similar organic structures on Terra. Third, I want a preliminary appreciation of farming potential—Terran style, with conventional cereals, vegetables and so on."

"All that will take time," observed Maeve O'Brien.

"Time is what you have plenty of," snapped Conrad. "Use it, but don't waste it . . . Maleter, we don't need

62

your particular skills just yet. Therefore you will assist Norstedt. I want three exo-skeletons unshipped, assembled, tested and operational as soon as we have clearance from Robinson and O'Brien about the air. You can have two robots to assist. O.K.?"

Gunnar Norstedt smiled. "O.K., by damn, Commander. It is good to hef work to do. We will unship the exos fast."

"Fine. We all have our assignments. If you have any spare time, use it to make sure your muscles are adjusted to Argus G."

*   *   *

It was midday, local time, before Maeve O'Brien and Mirlena Robinson gave their unqualified verdict on the atmosphere of Argus. The air sample had yielded a variety of micro-organisms, pollens and dust; but analysis had shown that there was nothing toxic in the air. Indeed, the atmosphere was better and purer than that of any comparable region on Terra.

By that time, the robots had hooked up the vids, set up an electrified defence perimeter and had established that there were no dangerous life-forms within it. The soil of Argus was rich in nitrogen-fixing bacteria, thus indicating that Terran colonists would be able to use conventional farming methods and develop independent food supplies within one planetary cycle.

Conrad was still worried. It all seemed too good to be true. There had to be a joker in the pack. He went dirtside as soon as O'Brien and Robinson had given clearance. He walked a few metres away from the scorched area of touch-down and gazed incredulously down at the green sward. The grass was just like the grass of Earth and, goddammit, there were even daisies. Genuine Earth-type daisies. He was amazed. A butterfly drifted past. He was even more amazed.

He glanced up at the towering column of the *Santa Maria*. Its skin was pitted and scarred by the impact of micro-meteors and by the heat stress of numerous lift-offs and touch-downs. But it was still a beautiful vessel—the more so because it had a known history. This is how happily married men must feel about their wives, he thought, when they become grey-haired and wrinkled. Then he scratched his silver eye-patch irritably. "Dammit," he said aloud, "I am not married to a bloody starship!"

Tibor Maleter came down the nylon ladder, followed by a robot. Gunnar Norstedt and another robot began to lower exo-units from the entry-port.

Tibor sniffed the air with satisfaction. "It's a lovely day, Commander. What we really need are deck chairs and some chilled lagers."

"What you need," snapped Conrad, ashamed of his own recent sentimentality, "is to get those exos operational fast."

"Yes, sir." Tibor looked hurt.

Conrad used his transceiver to call the nav deck.

"Lieutenant Smith, do you read me?"

"I read you, Commander."

"How does it look from up there?"

"Fine. The vids are functioning O.K. The perimeter defence is alive. I have three hundred and sixty degrees surveillance. Visibility and resolution are good—approaching ten kilometres. No signs of significant animal life. How is it dirtside?"

"Very pleasant. I have discovered daisies and a butterfly."

"Lucky you. Maybe Kurt is right. Maybe this is the Garden of Eden."

"The Garden of Eden contained a serpent," retorted Conrad. "Thus demonstrating the universality of Finagle's Second Law. Over and out."

*   *   *

A late lunch was taken in the saloon, in two sittings. Prior to relieving Lieutenant Smith at the command screens, Conrad took his meal with Kwango, Mirlena Robinson and Maeve O'Brien.

Apart from the routine tasks of unshipping equipment and analysing bio-samples, the long morning had been uneventful. Birds had been seen in the distance, but none of significant size. No ground animals had yet put in an appearance; but Mirlena Robinson had managed to acquire a number of insects for study—including Conrad's butterfly.

Kwango's report had been a model of brevity—largely because there was very little to report. Argus seemed to be amazingly normal so far. The various grasses and flowers were remarkably similar to many of those found on Earth, as were the small insects—ants, spiders, worms and the butterfly—that had already been examined. The worms of Argus, in particular, were almost identical to the worms of Earth. Their size, segmentation, methods of ingestion and reproduction indicated a parallel pattern of evolution. Which, as Mirlena Robinson explained, was only to be expected on a planet where the carbon cycle functioned *exactly* as it did on Earth.

"Presumably, we shall find considerable variation in the higher life-forms?" asked Conrad.

Mirlena smiled. "Inevitably, Commander. Even if the mineral content of Argus were an exact duplicate of that of Terra, the slight variation in G and the considerable variation in geological structure would alter the evolutionary pattern significantly."

"Gobbledegook," said Conrad, finishing his coffee. "I wish you scientists wouldn't cover your meaning in a string of bloody long words. What you are saying is that, despite the reassuring presence of cosy little earthworms, Argus is going to yield a few surprises. Right?"

"Right, Commander."

"They don't have to be nasty surprises, Boss," ventured Kwango.

"I wasn't aware that I had asked for your opinion, Kurt."

"You didn't, Boss." Kwango grinned. "But, sure as hell, there always comes a time when you need it."

"So this is not the time. I am going to relieve Lieutenant Smith at the screens. When you see Norstedt and Maleter, tell them I want the chopper and the hovercar unshipped and operational at least three hours before sunset. I want to take a good look at this demi-paradise."

Maeve O'Brien said: "You can't use both vehicles, Commander. Why the hurry?"

Conrad sighed. "Use your loaf, O'Brien. I'll take the chopper. The hovercar is a backup in case I come unstuck."

Mirlena Robinson said: "I think Kurt is probably right, Commander. It seems unlikely that we will encounter any major problems."

"Bless you, my child," retorted Conrad drily. "I hope *you* are right. I'm naturally cautious. Indulge me. It is a sign of age."

Mirlena stuck out her breasts. "Don't worry too much, Commander. It is bad for your blood pressure."

"Take care of yourself, Robinson. That is all I ask. I'll take care of me and my blood pressure."

Six hours later, Argus made the first strike.

Six hours later, Mirlena Robinson, black and beautiful, found out about Argus the hard way.

Phase Two

Death in the Grass

The day continued to be fine and warm, the sun pouring down its heat through a cloud-flecked sky. The heat was not unbearable, but it was enough to produce sweat stains on the coveralls of any who had to indulge in strenuous activity dirtside. Which meant, chiefly, Tibor Maleter and Gunnar Norstedt. They had let the robots do most of the heavy work, unshipping and assembling the exos and then unshipping the chopper and the hovercar. But Norstedt was the kind of engineer who did not trust robots too much. He and Maleter checked their work carefully, inspecting linkages, connections, servo-mechanisms, power sources and control systems. Movement in itself was sufficient to make them feel hot and sticky. Nevertheless, they had the chopper and the hovercar operational nearly four hours before sunset. They felt rather pleased and very thirsty.

Conrad came down from the nav deck. Lieutenant Smith had once more taken over at the command screens. Kwango and Mirlena Robinson were already dirtside. Kwango had been inspecting the perimeter defence and the gate mechanism; and Mirlena had been looking for more interesting specimens of insect life.

Conrad glanced at the chopper, and turned to Norstedt. "You have checked all systems?"

Norstedt looked pained. "Commander, I am a very good engineer. Is why you choose me, is it not? Exos, chopper and hovercar are all tuned for optimum performance. Tibor and me, we make sure bloody robots fix every damn hook-up perfectly."

Conrad grinned. "You have both done well. Thanks. If you go topside, you will find that Mark has been programmed to deliver two Carlsberg Specials, ice-cold, dew on the glasses, to the saloon about five from now. You look as if you could use them."

A great smile creased the face of the big Swede. "By bloody damn, Commander, you sure look after the peasants."

Conrad was nonplussed. "As a matter of interest, Gunnar, where did you learn your English?"

Norstedt shrugged. "In jail, Commander, from a West German dope dealer who could speak seven languages with some affliction." He looked puzzled. "My accent is bad?"

"No. Your phrasing is sublime. Go and hit the lager. Mark will accept one re-order only. I know your drinking history."

Norstedt saluted. "You do me too much honour, Commander. Your munificence is cunningly extrapolatic."

That left Conrad fazed. While he was trying to think of something to say, Norstedt and Maleter went topside to home in on the Carlsberg Specials.

Kwango came up. "Boss, I'd like to take *Miss* Robinson for a stroll, if that is O.K. by you."

"*Miss* Robinson?" enquired Conrad with a note of sarcasm.

"Boss, the lady, though black, is a lady. Cool the racist implications."

Conrad scratched his eye-patch irritably. "You have nothing better to do than take a stroll?"

"No, Boss."

It was on the tip of Conrad's tongue to make some acid remark and find something for Kwango to do. But he didn't, remembering that he owed the big black man a great deal—his life, for starters.

"O.K., Kurt. If *Miss* Robinson also has nothing better to do, you may both promenade. But take lasers and stay close enough to the perimeter for Lieutenant Smith to see you on the screens."

"Thanks, Boss. We'll be real careful." He turned to Mirlena. "What did ah tell you, honey chile? De good Commander sure has a heart o' purest gold."

Conrad sighed. "Don't press your luck. I'm going to lift north towards the mountains and see what I can see. I may take pix. There are at least three hours of daylight left, so I'll time the trip for around ninety minutes. I'll call the ship every fifteen. If I miss a call, Lieutenant Smith will call me. If I don't respond, you know what to do."

Kwango nodded. "Sure do, Boss. I seen it all before. But *please* don't bust any expensive equipment—and don't bust yourself up. So far it's been a nice day. Let's keep it that way."

Conrad did not trust himself to answer. He got into the chopper, started the vanes rotating and went immediately into maximum lift. As he shot skywards, he had the satisfaction of seeing that he had blown Kwango and Robinson flat on their backs. He went up to three hundred metres, circled the star-ship and looked down. All seemed shipshape. The exos were laid out side by side, like three reclining metal giants. A couple of robots—probably Luke and John—were erecting a duralumin storage hut for gear that would be needed dirtside; and the tiny figures of Kwango and Mirlena had become vertical again. Conrad smiled to himself, imagining the eloquent flow of language that would now be coming from the black genius. For a moment, he was tempted to drop low and blow them over again; but he resisted the impulse. Such pranks did not become the commander of a team of Expendables. He headed north towards the mountains.

Seven or eight kilometres from base, he saw a herd of quadrupeds grazing. He dropped to fifty metres and took telepix. They were big animals, rhinocerotic in shape, with disproportionately massive heads. He circled the herd slowly. The great creatures milled about, confused and angry at the noise of the chopper and their inability to get at it. Conrad noticed that about ten of the biggest animals took up defensive stations round the herd. Doubtless, they would be the bulls. He wondered if the quadrupeds would be a potential meal-supply for colonists. That would be something that would have to be looked into by Robinson and O'Brien. Suddenly, he had a mental picture of such a herd stampeding. If, by chance, they were to stampede towards the *Santa Maria*, they were large enough to go through the electrified defence perimeter as if it wasn't there.

Conrad made a mental note to get Kwango to locate a convenient supply of timber. Then, using the exos, he, Norstedt and Maleter could build a stockade round the perimeter. Or maybe, it would be less time-consuming to scoop out a deep ditch and possibly fill it with water. In any case, a local water supply would be useful. Tomorrow, Conrad decided, Maleter could get busy with his seismic gear and find out where the nearest water supply was. Then the robots could sink a well with sonic drills. Two for the price of one! A local water supply would reduce the demands on the *Santa Maria*'s recycling system.

While he was contemplating these possibilities, Conrad glanced at his electrochron and realized it was time to report back.

"*Santa Maria*, do you read me?"

"I read you, James. All is well?"

Conrad scratched his eye-patch irritably. "Dammit, Lieutenant, do not call me James. We are both on duty."

Indira's voice became slightly chilly. "Message received, Commander. Print-out shows you to be about seven point six kilometres due north. I can even see a dot that looks like the chopper on the screens. What has slowed you down?"

"I've found a herd of quadrupeds herbivores. Big bastards. Aggressive. Built like tanks, or king-size rhinos. It occurred to me that if they decided to come south, they could charge through our perimeter as if it were paper. But they could be a useful meat supply. We'll look into that later. Meanwhile, I'll drive them further north."

"O.K., cowboy, have fun. Over and out."

"Blast you, Smith," said Conrad angrily. "When on duty, you will preserve a proper respect."

There was no answer.

Conrad, still fuming, took the chopper down to ten metres and came in at the herd from the south. The bulls were courageous. They stood their ground, pawing and snorting until he was less than thirty metres from them. Then, apparently, they decided that discretion was the better part of valour. They roared in unison, the roars being loud enough to penetrate the chopper's bubble. At this signal, the entire herd turned and stampeded north.

Conrad chased them. He chased them well away from the *Santa Maria*.

*   *   *

Kwango and Mirlena were about a hundred metres outside the defence perimeter. They turned and looked back at the towering star-ship, smooth, phallic, beautiful.

Kwango felt a sudden surge of affection for the *Santa Maria*. "That old tin can has knocked the hell out of a lot of light-years. It has scored a lot of firsts, too . . . I'd hate to be the guy who has to tell Conrad she's going to be junked."

Mirlena was surprised. "Is the ship going to be scrapped?"

Kwango nodded. "That's what I heard back on Terra. The clever boys have something bigger and better on the

70

drawing board. Also they are working on a faster matter transmitter. So some genius figured that if you used a bigger ship, doubled the size of the team and threw in more exos and robots, you could cut costs, prove planets in half the time and pipe in the colonists at about three times the present rate."

"Does Conrad know about this?"

Kwango shrugged. "I don't know, baby. He hasn't mentioned it. But I wouldn't want to be around when he gets the official say-so."

Mirlena noticed a long thin, blue-green shiny strand—rather like thin wire or nylon cord—lying on the grass. She touched it with the toe of her boot. Nothing happened. Another strand lay close by it. She touched that also. Again nothing happened. Almost certainly, the strands were organic—possibly some kind of specialized grass or even fungus—but they looked inert, dead.

"Conrad has a history of violence, hasn't he?"

"He sure has. And busting the face of the late Director of ExPEND has improved his track record somewhat. When we get back to Terra, certain people will have sharpened some very long knives."

"Is he racist?" asked Mirlena suddenly.

"Why do you ask that, Mirlena?" For once, Kwango was nonplussed.

"He knocked us flat when he lifted off. Did he do it on purpose?"

"Yes, he did it on purpose."

"Then he must be racist. What a pity."

"Yes, Mirlena, he's a racist." Kwango grinned. "The secret is out. He doesn't like black, he doesn't like yellow, and he only goes for brown when it happens to be Lieutenant Smith. That white trash bastard is just naturally racist—human racist. He's for people. That's all."

"Then why did he flatten us?"

"Because I'm Kwango and because he is Conrad. Does that make sense?"

"No." Mirlena smiled. "But I'll think about it."

"Think about this also. If he ever needs a blank cheque signed Kwango, I'll give it. If I ever need a blank cheque signed Conrad, he'll give it. Now do you understand?"

Mirlena smiled. "Kurt, I know you are very clever, but perhaps you are also naïve. Let's change the subject. What do you think about these organic filigrees?" She pointed down at the blue-green strands lying in the grass.

Kwango knelt down. "Seems to be quite a lot of them half-hidden in the grass. They aren't quite parallel. From the way they are lying, I'd say they have a central source —all part of the same plant, probably."

Mirlena crouched beside him. "I'll take a sample back and put it under the microscope." But though the strands were very thin and looked fragile, she could not break one. "Even more interesting."

Kwango tried also, and failed. "*If* this stuff is organic, it is really tough . . . There has to be a purpose." Eventually, he managed to cut a piece off with a pocket knife, but he had to saw at it hard.

Mirlena put it in her coverall pocket. "Thanks. Now there's a mystery. It's limp, flexible and as tough as steel wire."

"It sure is, baby." Kwango felt the blade of his knife. "This vanadium steel has taken a beating."

Mirlena picked up another strand and pulled on it hard, lifting it clear of the grass. It was attached to what looked like a small blue mushroom or toadstool about three metres away. As she pulled, the blueness of the plant seemed to intensify.

"Well, well," said Kwango. "This cosy little planet has its surprises, after all." He, too, picked up a strand and pulled hard. Again the colour of the mushroom deepened.

Mirlena grew excited. "Kurt, this is a very complex plant—the most interesting thing we have found today. I want it for investigation."

"If the roots are only half as tough as these things," said Kwango, tugging on his strand and failing to break it or even shake the "mushroom", "we're going to have problems. That thing looks as hard as rock. I'll call a robot to come and lift it."

"Nonsense," said Mirlena. "The robot might damage

it too much. I can't see any more of these things around, so we will have to treat it carefully. I'll take a closer look. It may be possible to take a segment if I can't lift it all."

The "mushroom" seemed to become almost luminously blue as she stepped over the thickening carpet of threads.

"Mirlena," said Kwango, a note of anxiety in his voice, "I think we should leave it for remote——" He was going to say "handling", but the word died on his lips.

As Mirlena reached the mushroom, there was a tremendous whoosh! Kwango was almost thrown off his feet as the few threads on which he was standing—along with the hundreds of other fine strands attached to the mysterious plant—recoiled spirally like whirling whiplashes and wound themselves so tightly round Mirlena that the contours of her lovely body seemed now to be perfectly moulded in a cocoon of fine blue-green wire.

She screamed.

"Kurt! Help me! Help—ugh!" Her face contorted in agony, her eyes rolled, her mouth opened wide and her tongue protruded. She fought hopelessly for breath as the strands tightened their grip, forcing all the air out of her lungs.

Kwango rushed forward and tried to tear at the strands with his fingers.

Useless! They gripped Mirlena like spring steel.

She made a last feeble effort to draw breath, then her eyes closed and her head slumped forward. The cocoon of strands reached as high as her breasts and shoulders. But her throat was just clear of the deadly web. Though she was now unconscious, the plant still held her upright, the lethal strands visibly tightening their hold.

Kwango wasted no more time on the immovable strands. He stepped back, grabbed his laser rifle. But where the hell to burn?

He couldn't burn the strands because then he would burn Mirlena. A couple of crucial seconds passed before he realized that she had actually been lifted up to the head of the mushroom. Unconscious or worse, she was poised on it dead centre. Almost twenty-five centimetres of its thick stem or stalk lay exposed.

He burned. Maximum power. He burned.

The stem/stalk steamed, smoked, flared, severed.

Mirlena, still cocooned, fell heavily and lay still.

Kwango dropped the laser rifle and rushed to her.

Now he was able to tear the baleful strands from her crushed body. He pulled her clear of them. The strands had already cut her clothes to ribbons and made dreadful weals on her body.

Frantically, he tore the strips of clothing away and listened to her heart. No sound. Irrationally, he shook her. She remained limp. He listened again. No heartbeat. No sound of breathing. No anything. She was dead.

He cradled her in his arms for a few more precious seconds. Then he came to his senses. He fumbled in his coverall for the transceiver.

"Mayday! Mayday! Mayday! Come in *Santa Maria*, for christsake! This is Kwango. Get here fast, Lieutenant, and bring miracles. Mirlena is dead."

It was Matthew who answered. "Lieutenant Smith is already on her way, Mr. Kwango. The incident was observed on the screens. Estimated arrival time one point five minutes plus or minus 10 per cent. Kiss of life recommended. Do you read me?"

"I read you. Over and out,"

The kiss of life! Kwango cursed himself. He was slipping. Why hadn't he thought of that?

Even as these thoughts flashed through his mind, Kwango was already going into action

He pinched Mirlena's nostrils and forced her mouth wide open with the other hand Then he took a deep breath, placed his open mouth over hers and blew like hell. He pressed hard on her chest to make her exhale. Then he repeated the performance. And repeated it and repeated it. On the tenth go, Lieutenant Smith arrived in the hovercar. It was piloted by Mark.

Indira leaped out with her medikit before the machine had grounded. She came running.

"How goes it, Kurt?"

"No response. She's still dead." There were tears on Kwango's face.

Indira had a hypo ready. She said coldly: "Pull your-self together, you black bastard. We have work to do." She shot the adrenalin into Mirlena.

Kwango was surprised. "Indira, you sound just like *him*."

"What do you expect? He left me in command. I'm damned if I will report a casualty when he gets back . . . The adrenalin isn't working. Get that hovercar nearer."

"Why, Lieutenant?"

"Kwango, you are slipping. Get two leads on to the generator. I want to give her about two hundred and fifty volts. Move, man!"

While Kwango got the hovercar in position, Lieutenant Smith gave the kiss of life and worked expertly on the chest. There was still no response from Mirlena. Sweat dripped from Indira's forehead, falling on Mirlena's face, making rivulets on the smooth black skin.

"Juice available and ready, Commander." Kwango held out the leads. His voice was calmer now.

Indira took the insulated leads without a word. She studied Mirlena's bare breasts for a moment or two. Then she chose her spots and touched just below the breasts with both terminals. The body arched, and Indira snatched the terminals away. But then it sagged again. Indira listened for a heart-beat. There was none.

"Call Matthew. Tell him to get ready for a fast chill. If nothing else works, I'll try for a transplant."

"Right, Lieutenant."

While Kwango called the *Santa Maria*, Lieutenant Smith tried again with the electrical jolt. Again the body arched and flopped. Again nothing.

"If I knew enough about the bugs of Argus," said Indira angrily, almost to herself, "I'd open up and gamble on massage."

In a surge of impotent rage, she pressed down the termi-nals again on the smooth black flesh. The body jerked, muscles contracted, the dead limbs trembled with an eerie semblance of life. Indira held the terminals firmly in place.

Suddenly, there was a weak but unmistakable groan. Indira snatched the terminals away and flung them down.

75

They shorted with a noisy flash and blew the generator fuse.

She didn't care. She was listening for the heart. She heard it, felt it. Weak at first, erratic, then steady. The chest heaved as Mirlena Robinson took a deep breath and groaned again.

The eyes opened, rolled and then focused. "What happened?" she asked in a weak voice.

Lieutenant Smith said nothing. She listened to the heart once more. Finally, she lifted her head. "You'll live, Robinson. I've just cheated the devil. Now hear this: Don't say anything, don't do anything, don't think anything. Just lie still. We'll get you back to the ship and I'll examine you properly."

Kwango was exuberant. He flung his arms round Lieutenant Smith and kissed her. "Indira, you are the greatest! You are one hell of a woman!"

"Kurt," said Indira with a grim smile, "you may be the resident genius, but you are the most stupid genius I have ever met."

"Yes, Ma'am."

"And don't ever call me Ma'am!"

"Yes, Ma—Lieutenant. Permission to say: I love you?"

"Permission denied. Get the stretcher out of the car. I want Robinson in the intensive care unit five from now."

"Decision noted. Execution proceeds."

Matthew called from the nav deck. "Commander Conrad reported from the helicopter five point eight minutes ago. He asked to speak to Lieutenant Smith or Mr. Kwango. I apprised him of the situation. He is returning with all possible speed."

"Oh, my Gawd!" said Kwango appalled.

Phase Three

Another of Kwango's Tangos

"So Argus was going to be a holiday!" Conrad's voice had a nasty edge of sarcasm mingled with anger. "And you were going to pick a nice spot for sun-bathing!"

Kwango shrugged. "I'll save you the trouble, Boss. I am a stupid black bastard. It's a majority verdict."

Conrad was not to be placated. "Kwango, you are worse than that," he roared. "As an imbecile genius, you have to be unique. Why the hell didn't you stop her? You ought to know by now that in this business, things are never quite what they seem and are invariably worse than suspected."

Kwango tried to cool it. "Congratulations, Boss," he said lightly. "You just formulated a new cosmic constant, hereby defined as Conrad's First Law. I like it. Things are never quite——"

"Why the hell didn't you stop her?"

Kwango shrugged. "Boss, I offered to call a robot to lift that damn thing. But Mirlena wasn't in the mood for waiting. She moved in before I could stop her."

Conrad's voice became gentle, and that was even worse. "Kwango, you are a veteran, Robinson is an amateur. If, in your professional opinion a robot should have been used, you should have issued the necessary commands both to the robot and to Robinson. Because of your incompetence, we almost lost our biologist. That would have been a bloody fine start! And on our first day!"

"Yes, Boss."

"And don't call me Boss!" thundered Conrad. "We'll have some discipline around here." He raised his prosthetic arm menacingly. "Otherwise, I'll make a *pâté* out of what passes for your brain."

77

"Sorry, Commander."

"So you ought to be. For dereliction of duty, Kwango, I fine you one booze ration. Dismissed."

Kwango stood to attention. "Sir. Thank you, sir." He turned to go.

Conrad scratched his silver eye-patch irritably. He realized he had been over-reacting.

"Kwango!"

"Yes, sir."

"Cancel statement. It's been a hard day. We have all learned something—chiefly that Argus is not going to be a joy ride. O.K.?"

Kwango smiled. "O.K., Boss. I goofed. You had a right to scream."

They were in Conrad's cabin.

"Kurt, you know where the brandy is. Get it. You and I have some thinking to do."

"Yes, suh, Massa Boss. I allus knew you was a real white man."

Conrad sighed. "*Please.* That Uncle Tom crap is bad for my blood pressure, as you well know."

"Boss, I truly am sorry. I guess there is a stupid little demon in me that——"

"Belay explanations. I've heard 'em all."

At that point, Indira came into the cabin.

"Make it three glasses, Kurt." He turned to Lieutenant Smith. "What of the patient?"

"Multiple weals, multiple bruises, two cracked ribs and shock. She'll live."

"Sit down and join us, Lieutenant. I trust you, too, will now believe that Argus is going to be rough."

"How did you know, James?"

Conrad grinned. "I didn't know—and don't call me James. It is bad for discipline."

Kwango poured the drinks.

"Make them larger, Kurt. We are going to need immoral support."

Kwango raised an eyebrow and shot three more doubles into the brandy glasses.

"Boss, are we going to get smashed?"

"No, my friend. We are going to get sensible . . . Up in orbit you quoted Humphrey Bogart. I checked with the computer. It was from a twentieth-century movie melodrama. Now it is my turn." He raised his glass. "I give you Damon Runyon."

Kwango raised his glass. "Who is Damon Runyon, Boss?"

"Who was," corrected Conrad. "An obscure early twentieth-century writer. He left hardly anything but a memorable quote, which is: With human beings, the odds are five to two against."

Indira was puzzled. "Against what?"

"Just against," said Conrad. "But if Runyon could have known about Argus, he would have quoted larger odds against."

Kwango sighed. "Don't rub it in, Boss. I got the message the moment Mirlena hit the go button. What you are suggesting is that it would be statistically absurd for us to hit the only nasty surprise on our first day. Right?"

"Right." Conrad sipped his brandy. "Argus looks too good to be true. Therefore, it has a sting. We have merely received—if you will forgive mixed metaphors—a warning shot across our bows. Now hear some more bad news. The quadrupeds I saw from the chopper were two-tonne monsters that could go through our defence perimeter like a dose of salts if they decided to charge. I drove them further north to give us a clear night—I hope. But they—or another herd—could easily come down on us. So our immediate priority is to secure the safety of this vessel and our base. Recommendations?"

"A stockade," suggested Indira. "Just like the one we had on Zelos."

"How far away is the nearest timber, Kurt?"

"About thirty kilometres south. It's a long way to go for cocktail sticks."

"I agree. What about a ditch, then?' '

"A ditch is good," said Kwango. "If it's deep enough and wide enough it has to stop anything heavy."

"Good thinking," said Conrad drily. "Also the soil scooped out of the ditch can be used for earthworks. Also, if we can tap a good supply of water, the ditch can be turned into a moat."

"Good thinking," echoed Kwango, downing the last of his brandy. "I won't like what I'm about to hear."

Conrad smiled. "No, Kurt, you won't. At daybreak, you, Maleter and Norstedt will harness up into the exos. You will scoop out a ditch three metres from the electrified perimeter. The ditch will be three metres wide and two metres deep. The soil removed will be used for external earthworks two metres high. You will not, of course, continue the ditch and earthworks across the perimeter gateway. While all this is going on, O'Brien will take the hovercar and laser any and all of those funny blue mushrooms within a radius of ten kilometres. At the same time, I will have a couple of robots drilling for water so that we can fill your ditch. Skol!" Conrad raised his glass.

"Boss," said Kwango sadly, gazing at his empty glass. "I've run out of brandy."

"So you have, Kurt, so you have." Conrad's voice was sarcastic. "That is your second error of judgment today." He sipped some more and smacked his lips appreciatively. "Do you know how much it cost the taxpayer to put this Hennessy XO on Argus?"

Kwango sighed. "Permission to go and hang myself, Commander?"

"Permission granted—when I have finished drinking."

Lieutenant Smith took pity on the black man. "Medical prescription, Kurt. Two ounces of seventy proof to be taken slowly."

Conrad glared at her. "Lieutenant, I will decide who drinks what, where and when."

"Commander, as medical officer, I have the right to prescribe for my patient."

"Kwango is not your patient."

"I say he is. He has been in shock."

Conrad snorted. "In shock! That stupid black bastard doesn't even have a central nervous system."

Lieutenant Smith ignored him. "Kurt, you may draw the brandy from medical supplies." She gave Conrad a frosty glance. "Commander, my professional judgment has been challenged. I request that this be noted in the log."

"The hell with another brandy," said Kwango. "The price is too high."

"Damnation!" roared Conrad. "Pour yourself another drink, Kwango. At least, it will get this bloody woman off my back."

"I don't want another drink."

"Dammit to hell, that is an order! I will remind you that if you refuse to obey a lawful command, which this is, you can be charged with mutiny."

Kwango shrugged and reached for the bottle. "Thank you, Commander, sir, for the gracious hospitality. May I freshen your glass?"

Conrad caught the look in Indira's eyes and suddenly realized that he was being ridiculous. "Cancel previous statements," he said. "I'm sorry. Am I really as bad as that?"

Indira held out a hand. Conrad took it.

"Yes, James. You are. Kurt and I both know what it's all about."

Conrad sighed. "Yes, I suppose you do." Suddenly, he became intense. "I know Argus is going to be tough. I feel it in my bones. But we *are* going to prove this bloody planet. We have a good track record. So we are going to score one more for stupid *homo sap*. We'll last the cycle, and some of us will live to watch colonists popping out of the meat machine. That's all there is to it."

"I'll drink to that," said Indira, raising her glass.

"So will I," said Kwango. He grinned. "Boss, you know we always play it your way when the shooting starts."

"The shooting has started. We almost lost one on the first day . . . When will Robinson be fit for duty, Lieutenant?"

"Light duty?"

"Yes."

"Tomorrow."

"Good. She can monitor the screens."

Indira emptied her glass. "Tomorrow, Commander, you will report to me before you leave the *Santa Maria*."

"What the devil for?"

"I want to check your blood pressure."

"Goddammit!" he exploded. "I have too much to do."

"That is why I want to check your blood pressure," said Indira calmly. "Now, are you going to go to bed peacefully, or do I have to give you a shot?"

Conrad did not trust himself to speak.

"Good night, James," said Indira serenely. "Stop worrying. Matthew is on the screens, Mark, Luke and John are patrolling the perimeter, armed with lasers. The vids are functioning. Peter and Paul are engaged in maintaining ship systems. And by now, the rest of the team will have hit the sack. *Stop worrying.*"

Kwango downed the last of his brandy. "Good night, sweet prince. May angels sing thee to thy rest."

"Hamlet," snapped Conrad. "Are you trying to prove something?"

"Yes, Boss. I just proved it. You are not as illiterate as was formerly supposed."

He left hurriedly, before Conrad could throw anything.

*　　　*　　　*

Kwango in an exo-skeleton was sheer poetry in motion. He used the atomically-powered anthropomorphic machine as if it was simply an extension of himself.

The exo-skeletons were eight metres long from control crown to feet. They looked like king-size robots with slender, powerful limbs; but without a man or woman in the control harness, they were just pieces of inert and superbly complex engineering.

But with someone like Kwango in harness, an exo could do the work of a bulldozer, a crane, an excavator, a team of lumberjacks, a road construction gang or an armoured assault commando unit. An exo could be used to run across uneven terrain at 70 k.p.h., pluck up trees as if they were daisies, or dig ditches faster than fifty men with old-fashioned picks and shovels.

After an early breakfast, Kwango, Maleter and Norstedt went dirtside and harnessed up. The Hungarian and the big Swede had already had basic training in the use of exos; but they had yet to be educated in using the machines Kwango-style.

When they had harnessed up and had taken the exos carefully through the perimeter gate, Kwango gave them a radio briefing.

"Tibor, Gunnar, I know you have had the theory and some practice; but don't yawn too much if I remind you of the basic data. When you are in harness, any movement you make is amplified by a factor of fifty. It makes you feel godlike—and you are godlike. But only in a mechanical sense. Don't over-react, don't apply more power than you need. Take it easy. Otherwise, you got problems . . . Now, the good Commander, in his wisdom, has decided that we need a ditch, the specifications of which you already know. For us poor humans, the ground out here is pretty hard. Ain't been no rain, I suspect, for quite a while. But to your exo-fingers it is going to seem like wet sand. All you have to do is pretend that you are children at the seaside scooping out the sand for when the tide runs in. Watch me."

Gunnar said: "Kurt, we hef used these things before on Terra. We know what to expect."

Kwango laughed. "O.K., Gunnar. You start the ditch."

Gunnar Norstedt carefully took his exo down on its knees and started scooping with both tungsten steel hands. Almost immediately the exo fell flat on its control crown.

"Haw, haw," said Kwango. "You all right, Gunnar?"

"A bruised ego only, by damn," said Norstedt.

"So pick yourself up, man, and observe the expert."

Kwango took his own exo down on its knees. He used one of the massive exo-hands to brace the machine, by resting the hand on the ground so that there was three-point support for the exo.

With the other hand, he started to scoop up the soil in fifty-kilo handfuls and toss it expertly into place for the earthworks. He worked so quickly that to Tibor and Gunnar it looked as if an uninterrupted shower of soil and rocks was rising out of the ditch and piling up the earthworks in a supernatural fashion.

"By damn," said Gunnar. "I hef much to learn."

Tibor said: "How long can you keep this up, Kurt?"

"As long as I have to, white trash. If you two wonder boys can't match my pace, go get yourselves some coffee. I'll have it finished before midday."

Gunnar Norstedt gave a cry of rage. "You eruptive black egotist," he barked. "I vill do my share."

"So, also will I, superman," said Tibor.

Kwango stopped scooping. "O.K., bright boys, we'll make it a race. My next booze ration against half each of yours that I complete half the perimeter ditch before the pair of you finish the other half."

"Done!"

Tibor and Gunnar got their exos down in the position Kwango had used and started scooping away round the perimeter in the opposite direction.

Kwango watched them for a minute or two. "Make sure you keep to the specifications," he taunted. "De good Commander is fussy about such trifles."

Maleter swivelled his exo-crown and glanced back. "Why are you not working?"

"No hurry," said Kwango nonchalantly. "I'm only competing against amateurs."

"You will not lef—I mean laugh—ven ve trink your hooch," grunted Norstedt. His accent became atrocious when he was angry.

"No," retorted Kwango. "But I vill lef ven I trunk *your* hooch, turnip-head."

Kwango's mimicry was greeted by another cry of rage. "He who lefs last lefs bestest!" Norstedt continued scooping like one possessed.

Kwango laughed. "Gunnar, my friend, guess who is going to lof bestest. No prizes offered." Then he went to work, displaying that old Kwango magic. Every movement he made was at optimum efficiency. It was as if the exo had become a part of him—or he a part of it. The interface between machine and man was no longer definable.

*　　　*　　　*

After an early breakfast, Conrad went to the sick bay and inspected Mirlena Robinson.

"Now you know," he said laconically.

She gave a faint smile. "Yes, Commander. Now, I know. I'm sorry I was stupid. I'm sorry I caused such trouble."

Lieutenant Smith was there.

"I have checked her over again, Commander. When she has had breakfast, she can get up and monitor the screens, if you wish. But I don't want her upright for more than four hours at a stretch. Understood—sir?"

"Understood, Lieutenant."

"Also I don't want her placed in a stress situation. She aches like hell and the cracked ribs need rest."

"O.K., Lieutenant, message received." Conrad turned to go.

"Hold it, Commander!"

He tried to look surprised. "What's the problem, Lieutenant?"

"You have an appointment with a sphygmometer. Remember?"

Conrad let out a great sigh. "Damnation! Oh, well, get it over with quickly. I'm in a hurry."

Lieutenant Smith wound the inflatable tube round his arm, squeezed the air-pump bulb and used her stethoscope. Expertly, she noted the rise and fall of the column of mercury in the sphygmometer. She did it three times.

"As I thought, your pressure is significantly high, Commander."

"So?"

"So I know you don't have nephritis, and I do know something about your physical and psychological profile. You have hypertension."

"So?"

"If we were on Terra, I'd take you off active service for at least a month. I'd control your diet, regulate your sleep, relaxation and exercise. I'd keep you under surveillance, shoot you full of Reduction-B—which I don't have here—and quite possibly recommend a desk job."

"How nice." Conrad's tone was icy. "How nice it is that we are not on cosy old Terra, where you could doubtless get somebody with a lot of gold braid on his sleeves to believe that gobbledegook and sign me off. Fortunately, we are on Argus, taking a nice rest cure. And I would remind you that here I hold supreme authority."

"You do not hold supreme authority!" snapped Indira. "If in my professional opinion you are unfit for command, I can——"

"And am I unfit for command?"

"Not yet."

"Good. Then don't waste my time." He turned to Mirlena. "Robinson, you can take a spell on the screens an hour from now. Next time you go dirtside, don't get clever."

"Yes, sir."

"Commander," said Lieutenant Smith, "I'm giving you some pills and I want your assurance that you will take at least eight hours sleep every night and delegate as much authority as you can."

"Lieutenant, I will take the pills if they don't affect my performance. And that is all the nonsense I'll stand. Incidentally, I would like you to accompany O'Brien when she goes to clear the vicinity of those plants that tried to eat Robinson. Take a robot. See if those bloody things will react to a machine. But don't take any chances yourselves. When you have discovered whether or not they like robots as well, burn all you can find. That's all, I'm going dirtside."

"What if the robot gets trapped?" asked Indira.

"See if it can fight its own way out." He grinned. "At least you won't have to worry about giving it the kiss of life," he glanced maliciously at Mirlena, "or sticking electrodes under its poor bruised tits."

He left before either woman could say anything.

They looked at each other.

"Well," said Mirlena, "this is an aspect of the Commander I haven't seen before."

Lieutenant Smith said: "You have a lot to learn about Conrad. This is his way of putting us on our mettle. Last night, he tore strips off Kwango for allowing you to be taken by that carnivorous plant."

86

"But it wasn't Kurt's fault," protested Mirlena. "I was just being stupid."

"Conrad doesn't like stupidity. He couldn't vent his anger on you, so Kwango was the next best target."

"That man is a monster!" flared Mirlena.

"Yes," agreed Lieutenant Smith calmly. "He is a monster. But he gets things done. His way."

"He didn't have to put me on the screens. He could have assigned a robot. I ache everywhere."

"It is his way of punishing you."

"Male chauvinist pig!"

Indira lost her temper. "Get clever, Robinson. Your idiocy put the project at risk. Male chauvinst pig Conrad may be. But he knows how to prove planets."

Phase Four

Kwango Wins: Mark Doesn't Lose

By the time Conrad hit dirtside, Kwango had unharnessed. He was drinking one of the three cups of coffee he had called the robot Peter to deliver while the Nigerian was scooping out the last three metres of his stint.

"Are you letting the new boys do all the work?" asked Conrad.

Kwango looked pained. "Boss, I have done my half. About one minute from now, you will have your ditch complete and earthworks raised as required. Also, I shall have acquired an extra booze ration."

Conrad looked puzzled momentarily. Then he understood. He smiled. "They were silly enough to bet against you operating in an exo."

"Yes, Boss, they were that stupid."

"I don't think they will take any more bets."

Kwango shrugged. "It was a one-off."

"Are they any good?"

"Not bad. Compared to anyone else, they're not bad. Alas, they were up against Kwango."

Conrad sighed. "Cut the commercial. You've set it to music before."

Maleter and Norstedt had now joined up with Kwango's half of the ditch. They came inside the perimeter, laid their exos down alongside Kwango's and unharnessed.

"Come and get your coffee, friends," called Kwango. "It may be a little cold. I programmed it while taking out my last three metres."

Norstedt took defeat with good grace. "By damn, Kurt, you work like a crimson maniac. When I look up, I see you moving like the penumbral jiggernot in full cry."

"How's that again?" Kwango was fazed.

"Gunnar learned his English from a West German dope dealer who could speak seven languages with some affliction," explained Conrad gravely. "I thought you knew."

He turned to Maleter and Norstedt. "If Kwango ever wants to bet you that he can fly direct to heaven by just flapping his arms, don't take the bet."

Tibor smiled. "We have learned expensively, Commander, that Kurt is a man of great talent."

"Right," said Conrad. "Remember also that his talent is only slightly less than his ego."

There was a serious of loud explosions. The ground shook.

"What demonically is that?" Norstedt looked alarmed.

"Sorry, I should have warned you," said Conrad. "Luke and John have been assigned to seismic survey. I want a convenient water supply—to ease the load on our recycling system and possibly to turn the ditch into a moat."

He called Matthew on his transceiver. "Any results yet from the survey, Matthew?"

"Preliminary data indicates possible presence of water north north west of *Santa Maria*. Distance from vessel: three hundred and forty-five metres. Confirmatory print-out expected seven minutes from now, plus or minus 10 per cent."

"Upon confirmation, have Luke and John assemble drilling rig and commence drilling operations."

"Decision noted. Execution proceeds."

Conrad turned to Kwango. "Kurt, when you have finished gloating, take the chopper and go south. I want to know more about the terrain and more about the animal life."

"O.K., Boss. How far can I go?"

Conrad scratched his eye-patch. "Use your wits, man. Be back before nightfall. And bring some useful data."

Kwango rolled his eyes. "Dere ain't no peace for the godly."

"Nor is there any rest for the wicked," retorted Conrad. "Move, black man, and don't wreck expensive machinery."

Kwango opened his mouth to say something, then thought better of it.

*　　*　　*

By mid-afternoon, the robots had drilled down to pure water which did not need pumping and came whooshing up the drill stem under immense pressure. Until the well was capped, fountains rose fifty metres in the air, dazzling and beautiful in the late sunshine, creating a fine mist and a miniature rainbow.

The water was wonderfully cold and clear. Conrad had bottles of it taken to the lab for exhaustive tests. He felt reasonably certain that the Expendables would be able to use it; but he was not going to take any chances until O'Brien and Robinson had checked its mineral content and its bio-contents.

Conrad was looking forward to the simple pleasure of drinking cold fresh water. Theoretically, the *Santa Maria*'s recycled water was just as good; but somehow it tasted flat and slightly bitter, despite the 100 per cent efficiency of the filtration and distillation systems.

In any case, the star-ship was no longer a closed system, its occupants taking precious water—in the form of urine, sweat, exhaled vapour—with them whenever they left the ship. Conrad wanted to close down the recycling plant and have the Expendables eating and drinking the food and water of Argus long before it was necessary to break into reserve supplies.

Lieutenant Smith and Maeve O'Brien didn't find many of the lethal mushroom-like plants with their long strands fanning out, half-hidden in the grass. In fact only three were discovered within a radius of ten kilometres from the star-ship.

They had taken the robot Mark with them in the hover-car. When the first of the bluish mushrooms was sighted, about four kilometres to the south-west, Lieutenant Smith grounded the car a little distance away, and gave Mark his instructions.

"You see that small blue plant over there in the grass?"

"Yes, Lieutenant."

"I think it is the same kind of plant that almost killed Mirlena Robinson. I wish to test its reactions. I want you to approach it slowly."

"Decision noted. Execution proceeds."

Mark got out of the hovercar and moved slowly forward. Maeve O'Brien recorded the sequence with a vid camera, while Lieutenant Smith held her laser rifle and transceiver ready. Mark was less than half a metre from the centre of the plant when there was a whoosh as the hundreds of strands whipped up with fantastic speed and completely cocooned the heavy, man-sized robot.

Lieutenant Smith used the transceiver. "Do you read me, Mark?"

"I read you, Lieutenant."

"Have you suffered any damage?"

"Nil damage. All systems function. Vision zero because of biological matter covering video-sensing units."

"Raise your right arm."

"Decision noted. Execution proceeds."

There was a slight ripple of movement in the cocoon. It stopped. "Request permission to use maximum force, Lieutenant."

"Permission granted."

"Decision noted. Execution proceeds." There was a sound like glass shattering, then one of the robot's massive arms broke out of the cocoon. The broken strands curled up like antique watch springs.

"Now raise the other arm."

"Decision noted. Execution proceeds."

Again there was the bizarre sound of glass breaking as the robot's left arm emerged. Again the broken strands coiled themselves tightly. At the same time, the remaining tendrils fell away—as if, somehow, the plant sensed its impending destruction.

Indira said: "I want samples of this plant—the strands, the central stalk, the roots. Try to lift the stalk clear of the ground."

"Decision noted. Execution proceeds."

Mark bent his ponderous metallic body, gripped the mushroom-like growth and pulled. It came up easily. Immediately, there was what sounded like an ear-splitting human scream. The screams died. The mushroom-like plant in Mark's metallic hands deflated and shrivelled like the skin of a pricked balloon.

"My God!" exclaimed Maeve O'Brien. "Is it plant or animal?"

"Use your head, O'Brien," said Lieutenant Smith tartly. "The thing has roots. The scream was caused by loss of air pressure as Mark lifted it. We'll stow the samples and continue the search and destroy programme."

She recalled Mark to the hovercar. The outward-spiralling search continued. From there on, they simply lasered the plants when discovered.

Phase Five

The Piranha Bugs

That evening, over dinner, Conrad discussed the day's events. Kwango was not present; but he had radioed Matthew, who was on duty at the communications console, to announce that he would be touching down in fifteen minutes. It was barely dusk, and Conrad was not unduly worried. The chopper had an auto-pilot that was almost a built-in robot. If Kwango wished, he could hit the auto-button, utter the necessary instructions in plain language and go to sleep. The auto-pilot could touch-down safely in total darkness, dense fog and/or a Force Six gale.

"Much has been accomplished today," said Conrad. "I am grateful to all of you. We now have an adequate defence system. We have an independent water supply—tests have not yet been completed, but I am assured that in all probability we will be able to drink it as it is. If not, then we simply set up a distillation plant."

"Also, the dangerous plants have been eliminated from the required area, and their characteristics will presently be investigated. Fortunately, they do not appear to be numerous, but, in any case, a selective killer can be devised.

"During the next few days, we are going to consolidate our position and carry out intensive exploration. It is important to find adequate food sources, to assess their potential and to use them ourselves. I also want us to make a detailed geo-bio-survey of one thousand square kilometres and after that magnetometric and seismic surveys of selected regions."

It was at this point that Kwango came into the saloon.

"Hi, Boss. Anything interesting been going on back here at the ranch while I was away?"

Conrad scratched his silver eye-patch. "What kept you, Kwango? How far south did you get?"

Kwango sat down at the table. Almost simultaneously, the robot Luke brought his first course—a segment of Spanish honeydew melon.

"Mah goodness. That looks real temptin'." He attacked the melon with fervour.

"Your report, Kwango!" Conrad's voice indicated that he was not in the mood for funnies. He sensed that there was something wrong.

Kwango put his spoon down. "Sorry, Boss. I was delayed because I made some very interesting discoveries. I went about two fifty kilometres south. I took it slow and low—average altitude about sixty metres. And on the way, I took time off to laser some of those playful little plants that tried to convert the lovely Mirlena into digestible protein."

"Kurt," said Conrad. "I know you. And I know that you are about to shatter us with surprises. Do it quickly." He raised his prosthetic arm. "Or you will never live to eat your main course."

Kwango looked pained. "Boss, you are a hard man. Which do you want first—the bad news or the worse news?"

Conrad gave a grim smile. "Feed it to us in your own inimitable fashion, Kurt. But don't get clever."

"O.K., Boss. The worse news first. There are on this planet insects, flying creatures which look like king-size dragon flies, sound like hornets and operate like piranha. They come in swarms. They settle on anything that moves, and they eat it to the bone in five minutes flat. And how do you like that?"

"I don't. What happened?"

"I was observing a herd of the quadrupeds you saw yesterday. Then I heard one hell of a noise in the sky—louder than the chopper engine—and I looked up and it seemed as if a cloud was passing under the sun.

"Most of the herd was grazing. The chopper hadn't worried them too much because I kept at a discreet distance. But when they heard the sound of that cloud of flying things, those two-ton herbivores went mad. Instant stampede.

"The insects were coming in at about 30 k.p.h. and at an altitude of maybe twenty metres. So the quadrupeds stampeded roughly west, doing maybe 40 k.p.h."

Kwango scratched his head. "All of them took off except three of what looked like the bulls. Those critters just turned to face the swarm. They stamped and roared and shook themselves about just as if they were trying to get noticed."

"And were they?" asked Conrad.

Kwango nodded his head emphatically. "They sure were, Boss. That big swarm of flying things—it was about

93

seventy metres in diameter, and it was so dense it looked like a black cloud—registered the presence of the defiant bulls and promptly lost interest in pursuing the herd."

Kwango pushed his melon away. "Boss, after what I've seen, I don't feel too hungry this evening. But I sure would appreciate a very large brandy."

Conrad signalled to Luke. "One half litre Hennessy XO brandy, one half litre Ballantine whisky, seven glasses. Execute."

"Thanks, Boss," said Kwango. "This comes under the heading of emergency medical treatment."

"From what you have already said, it looks as if we are all going to need emergency medical treatment," observed Conrad grimly. "So Argus was going to be a joyride!"

"Boss, I will never tempt Providence again . . . Anyway, this is what happened. Before you could say knife, that black cloud transformed itself into a great torus— about a hundred metres in diameter. It was just as if all those thousands of flying things were controlled by a group mind function. Then the torus sank down to an altitude of maybe two metres to form a living, whirling fence around the trapped bulls."

Luke brought the brandy and the whisky. Lieutenant Smith poured a very large brandy and gave it to Kwango. He smiled at her gratefully, and raised the glass with a shaking hand.

"Make mine whisky," said Conrad. "The rest of you name your own tipple." Most of the Expendables settled for whisky. Indira poured generous measures.

Conrad downed his whisky in a single swallow. "Well, Kurt, let's have the *dénouement*."

Kwango coughed and spilled a little of his brandy. "It wasn't too nice, Boss. Those bulls had deliberately sacrificed themselves for the rest of the herd. One of them charged the flying torus. It got stopped in its tracks."

"How?"

"A group of the flying creatures zoomed out from the torus and completely covered its head. Within seconds the beast was shivering, trembling. Then suddenly it just heeled over. More of the insects detached themselves from

94

the torus, and pretty soon the body of the fallen bull was covered with them. As some rose—having eaten their fill, I guess—and returned to the whirling ring, more came in. It began to look like the entire operation was computer controlled." Kwango gulped more brandy. "Boss, within five minutes that two-tonne quadruped was a skeleton. I swear it . . . Then the ring tightened round the remaining bulls—which by this time were not too happy.

"One of them couldn't stand the waiting, I guess. He tried to break out, and got the same treatment . . . Now for the funny bit, Boss. Fasten your seat-belt."

"O.K., Kurt, give it to us neat."

"They played with the surviving bull. They played with it for all of twenty minutes. And when I say played, I mean they tormented and tortured the poor creature till it was lathered with sweat and out of its tiny mind. One group of insects would detach itself from the spinning torus and zoom in as if to attack its head. At the last moment, they would swerve and return to the torus. Then another group would come in and pretend to attack its flank. The poor animal would turn to meet them head on, and then they would sheer off. Then another group would make for its arse or its belly or its legs, and so on. Eventually, that two-tonne beast was a shaking, terrified psychiatric wreck, dead on its feet. It didn't care any more, didn't react when the creatures buzzed it fore, aft and amidships. It just stood there in total shock. When the flying things realized the party was over, they just came in and gave it the treatment. It was half-way to being a skeleton before it hit the deck."

"And then?" enquired Conrad.

Kwango tossed off his remaining brandy. "When they'd finished, those hell-spawned critters just rose up into the air and went into formation as before—the same globular cluster. They—it, possibly—looked as if they or it were not entirely satiated with recent entertainment and would shortly be looking for more fun and games."

Conrad replenished Kwango's glass. "So you took action."

Kwango looked surprised. "Yes, Boss. But how would you know?"

Conrad drank his whisky. "I know my Kwango. Tell it like it was."

"Well, I got mad. I decided that those bastard insects were presumptuous and were not going to have it all their own way. So I took the chopper straight into them and sliced the cloud in two. The vanes must have knocked out hundreds in my first pass. But they had regrouped by the time I swung round. I hit them again and again. Every time I went through them, hundreds or maybe thousands of dead or dying insects fell out of the sky.

"Pretty soon, they got the message." Kwango gave a faint smile. "Boss, that cloud—what was left of it—departed at about 50 k.p.h. So I grounded and went to have a look at the cemetery."

Conrad scratched his silver eye-patch. "You are not empowered to take unnecessary risks, Kwango. Some of those insects might have had a go at you."

"They did." Kwango grinned and tapped his head. "But I got it up here. I put on a suit before I got out of the chopper. As soon as I hit dirt, some of the insects that had only been stunned picked themselves up, got into an attack formation and came at me. Very droll! I snatched a few handfuls out of the air and popped them into one of them plastic, expanding specimen jars which are a marvel of modern science, and all that crap. Also quite droll. Once the little darlings knew they were boxed in, they got all uptight and stung themselves and/or their dear brethren to death. Quite instructive!

"Another brandy, Boss? Postively my final performance."

Conrad shrugged, and pushed the bottle towards him. "It seems to be your party, Kurt. Just don't get pissed out of your mind, because you have a lot of hard thinking ahead of you."

Kwango took the bottle gratefully, and nodded. "My sentiments, precisely, Commander. This here planet is suddenly beginning to scare the shit out of me."

Indira spoke. "Did you take a look at the dead quadrupeds?"

Kwango drank more brandy. "I did, dear Lady Lieutenant. Everything had been eaten except the bones, the contents of the stomach and colon. Dem flying piranha/scorpions had demselves a real ball. Having registered this fact, I returned to the chopper and went on my merry way."

Conrad said drily: "You have cheered us up enormously, Kurt. Now let's have the bad news."

"The bad news, Commander, is that there are primates at the bottom of our garden, not so very far away. In fact, about thirty-eight kilometres south west."

"Primates?"

"Bloody baboons!" shouted Kwango. Then he pulled himself together. "Sorry, Boss. Forgive me. It was a shock. There was this forest. It looked interesting. I grounded to take a look. Then out came the welcome committee. That was a surprise, too. They were not aggressive. Just inquisitive. It was mutual."

"How close did you get?"

"Maybe fifty metres. The next item of bad news is that they are tool users, and that they make the tools they use. You see, Boss, these creatures use *manufactured* tools. I saw them digging with spades. Also, they got language. I heard them talking to each other. Not random noises or identity-declarations, or sex advertisement sounds, or flight-or-fight stuff or any of the usual animal vocals. They made simple sentences, accompanied by gestures. All very interesting. I think I want to go to bed."

Conrad started to scratch his silver eye-patch, realized what he was doing and stopped. "Kwango, you will remain relatively sober, awake and alert. That is an order."

"Yes, Boss."

Mirlena Robinson spoke. "Kurt, could these baboon-like creatures be defined as people?"

Kwango laughed. "De sixty-four thousand solar question! I don't know. I need more time, more observation."

Tibor Maleter looked at Conrad. "How do we define people, sir?"

97

Conrad gave a grim smile. "Another sixty-four thousand solar question. According to the book, they are intelligent tool-using creatures with social organization and language."

Kwango hiccupped. "Score one, Commander. Using those criteria, the baboons are people. Ergo, we can't take their planet. Ergo we all go home. Very nice . . . Permission to go to bed and sleep it off?"

"Permission denied," snapped Conrad. He gazed at the rest of the Expendables. "We are here to prove Argus—one way or the other. Mankind needs new planets. Last time I was on Terra, a Third World economist told me—and backed his commercial up with figures—that it cost half a million lives in the underdeveloped countries to mount a single extra-solar proving operation. The money, energy and resources needed to put us here on Argus could have saved a lot of kids in South America, or India, or China, for a while at least.

"Therefore, we must be aware that there are damn near a hundred thousand ghosts on the back of each of us. So we do not abandon Argus unless we can show that mankind cannot colonize successfully or until most of us are dead.

"As of now, we are at battle stations. The screens will be monitored at all times by a human being. It is not that I don't trust Matthew and his merry band. But they have no significant decision-making capacity . . . Lieutenant Smith, you will work out a rota."

"Ay, ay, sir."

"Also," went on Conrad, "in view of what Kurt has told us about the flying piranha, no one will go outside the perimeter unless suited with helmet at the ready, laser-armed and accompanied by a robot or another Expendable.

"We'll break the command screens duty into six four-hour watches. Lieutenant Smith, draw up a rota. All of us except Kwango will take one watch every day."

"Ay, ay, sir."

"I get time off for good behavior?" enquired Kwango hopefully.

Conrad shook his head. "God help us, you are supposed

98

to be the brains of this outfit, Kurt. I want to know about those flying things fast. I want to know where they nest, roost, go to earth or whatever. I want to know how they breed, where they breed, when they breed and recommendations for taking them out. You will be assigned one robot for permanent duty and you will have priority use of the chopper or hovercar."

"Thanks, Boss, for nothing," said Kwango, sombrely. Suddenly he brightened. "Actually, I don't need a robot. I need a biologist. I need Mirlena."

"I'm sure you do," said Conrad with sarcasm. "Last time you operated with her, she nearly got killed . . . Anyway, she's needed here. There is a lot of work to be done on potential food sources."

"Commander," said Mirlena, "if we can't knock out these dangerous creatures, it's a waste of time discovering which animals and plants are edible."

"Maybe you're right," conceded Conrad grudgingly. "But if you are volunteering to back up Kwango, you will have to manage on less sleep. I want your schedule of investigations to proceed normally. Understood?"

"Understood, Commander."

"O'Brien, when will you be sure that the local water supply is O.K. for use?"

"Before midday tomorrow, Commander. I have already analysed the samples. But I want to run an integrity check on the first ten thousand litres."

"Good. The sooner we hook up, the better. After that, you put on your biochemist's hat and take some of the pressure off Robinson. I presume you can check the remaining samples for food value and toxicity?"

"That's part of my work, anyway, Commander."

"Good. We'll keep new samples coming . . . Maleter and Norstedt, in the morning, I want you to harness up and construct some large, tough cages—say about six. Use local timber. There is no need to drain our own resources. And set up the cages in a compound of their own. You can have robot help if you need it."

Norstedt grinned. "Ve need no robots, *Herr Kommandant*. The Kwango style is upon us."

Kwango rolled his eyes. "The Kwango style is unique, Gunnar. With considerable luck, you and friend Maleter might go for bronze."

Tibor Maleter said: "What are the cages for, Commander?"

"Political prisoners," snapped Conrad testily. "Use your loaf, man. I want samples of anything that stands on two, three, four or more legs. Including Kwango's baboons. After you have constructed the menagerie, you can go hunting—in exos. Use anaguns if you have to, but don't damage the animals." He yawned and stretched. "Well, it has been an interesting day. I trust you are all finally convinced that Argus is no longer the demi-paradise it was supposed to be. My recommendation is that we all go to bed early, bearing in mind that a continuous human watch must be maintained on the screens . . . Who is the first victim, Lieutenant?"

Indira smiled faintly. "You are, Commander."

"That figured," said Conrad. "Who relieves me?"

"I do."

Conrad could not resist the temptation. "You always have," he said.

Phase Six

Piranha Bug City

During the next few days, all the Expendables worked very hard—as did the robots. But the robots were not subject to fatigue, the Expendables were. And when human beings are overtired, they are apt to get careless. That was the point at which one of the Expendables died in a strange and gruesome fashion. But before tragedy struck, much had been accomplished.

The local water supply proved, not only to be harmless, but extremely beneficial. Maeve O'Brien's analysis showed that it contained trace minerals in similar proportions to those of the most noted spa waters of Earth. When drunk cold—as cold as it was when it gushed from deep below the planetary surface—the water was semi-sparkling and produced a heady sense of well-being. Better than Perrier water, or Vichy water, or the waters of Malvern or Buxton.

The *Santa Maria*'s recycling system was closed down. Good local water was available in abundant supply, meat was available—the rhinocerotic quadrupeds that Conrad had discovered yielded steak of excellent quality, and gazelle-like creatures whose meat was like venison had been observed to exist in abundance. Five edible plants had been discovered, analyzed and proved. They were like mushrooms, carrots, kale, apricots and blackberries. But not quite the same. There was a subtle difference. An Argus difference. It was intriguing.

Maleter and Norstedt constructed the menagerie and its compound from timber that had to be hauled more than thirty kilometres. The entire operation took more than two full days. Using the exos, it was easy enough to pull up young trees, snap off the root section and the top to the required length, and strip off the branches. The real problem was transporting them back to the *Santa Maria*. Gunnar Norstedt solved it by laser-felling a tree that was like a small sequoia and that had a trunk more than two metres in diameter near its base. Having dropped the tree, he expertly laser-sliced four sections from the trunk, each section approximately fifty centimetres thick. Using these sections as huge wheels, he and Maleter were able to construct a large cart or wagon capable of hauling more than fifty trimmed tree-trunks at a time. It was an impressive sight for whoever was on duty at the command screens when a wagon-load of timber, pushed with little apparent effort by Norstedt and Maleter in their exos, came rolling across the grassy plain at 15 k.p.h.

While Kwango and Mirlena Robinson were investigating the piranha bugs, Conrad and Lieutenant Smith used the hovercar alternately for detailed ground exploration. Conrad worked to the north and Lieutenant Smith to the south. Between them, they made some interesting discoveries. Apart from the two-tonne rhinotypes, already encountered, they found game in abundance—small, furry creatures like hares or rabbits; swift, graceful animals like deer; creatures that were remarkably similar to the terrestrial giraffe; a kind of wild pig; massive animals of about one tonne that had all the characteristics of the lowly hedgehog, including great timidity; even shaggy, miniture kangaroos and something that was three mitres tall, could run at 60 k.p.h., and looked like an ostrich or cassowary bird.

Oddly, no carnivores were discovered. Conrad was puzzled. With so many herbivores around, he would have expected animal predators—such as animals corresponding in their habits and needs to lions, tigers, jaguars or other flesh-eaters.

Lieutenant Smith gave special attention to the baboon colony that Kwango had found. This annoyed Kwango somewhat, since he seemed to regard the baboons as his own special property. But, as Conrad pointed out. Kwango's priority was to discover as much as possible about the piranha bugs, and to devise means of eliminating them. Unless that could be done, Argus could not be proved.

While the menagerie was being built; while Maeve O'Brien almost lived in the lab, working as chemist, biochemist and biologist, dissecting, analysing and classifying the specimens brought to her; and while Conrad and Lieutenant Smith extended their ground survey, Kwango and Mirlena Robinson ranged farther and farther afield in their quest for the piranha bugs. They found nothing at all on the first and second days of the search. They had systematically covered an area of ten thousand square kilometres, and nothing was to be seen. It was as if the piranha bugs had never existed.

But they did exist. Kwango had brought back the evidence to prove it. Seventeen dead bodies in a specimen jar.

Maeve—and Mirlena in her spare time—worked on them, discovering that the piranha bugs secreted a very concentrated kind of formic acid as well as a compound similar to curare.

On the third day, one hundred and fifty kilometres west of the *Santa Maria*, Kwango hit pay-dirt. He and Mirlena were cruising in the chopper at an altitude of about two hundred metres. Below them was a grazing herd of rhinotypes. Then, lo, from the west came a cloud no bigger than a man's hand. Except that it was a damn sight bigger when it got close up, and the piranha bugs registered the presence of the herd.

Kwango brought the chopper down low to an altitude of twenty-five metres. He held it hovering about two hundred metres downwind from the herd.

"Mirlena, we'll get this sequence on tape," said Kwango. "See what can be done with the tele-lens. I don't want to go in closer; but we need good resolution and detail."

"Will magnification 15 be O.K.?"

"Make it 20. Then later on, we can study the attack pattern in slow replay."

The herd's response to the deadly cloud, and the piranha bug's strategy was the same as before. Only this time, four bulls stayed for the sacrificial rearguard action. It was a bigger herd of rhinotypes. It was also a bigger cloud of piranha bugs. Kwango was interested.

"It looks like we got proportional representation, O best beloved," said Kwango.

Mirlena got the vid rolling, then turned to Kwango and stuck out her magnificent breasts. "What the hell does that mean, Kurt?"

"It means that the herd has a pretty good idea how many animals are going to satisfy the piranha bugs. And vice versa. This herd is about a third larger than the one I saw. This cloud of piranha bugs is about a third larger, too. Seems like there are good telecommunications on this planet . . . Please excuse the intrusion of privacy." He kissed her, and allowed a hand to fondle her breast. "Sex and violence just naturally go together, O best beloved."

Mirlena shivered, sighed, returned his ardour. "Kurt,

you are a most disconcerting man. What does this 'O best beloved' thing signify?"

Kwango smiled. "You never read Kipling, Mirlena? Shame on you! Ah, well, it's hard to make love in a chopper. We'd better concentrate on the floor show."

The ritual was as before. The torus of piranha bugs came down, trapped, tormented and finally destroyed the sacrificial bulls, then rose once more to form a great globular cluster.

Mirlena watched it all, and was sick. With great presence of mind, she managed to vomit into a plastic bag. Kwango took the bag and tossed it out of the chopper. He kissed Mirlena again, tasted the bitterness on her lips and was savagely glad. "You are not going to believe this, O best beloved, but we just made love."

"Kurt, you are crazy! What the hell do you mean? I feel so ashamed. I'm a biologist. I'm supposed to be inured to the kind of thing we have just witnessed. Goddammit, I'm an Expendable!" There were tears in her eyes.

"Cool it, little one," said Kwango tenderly. "First, you are a woman. Second, you are a biologist. Third you are with Kwango. So relax."

Mirlena pulled herself together. "I suppose we should go down and inspect the remains."

"No." Kwango pointed towards the cloud of piranha bugs. "We follow those bastards. They've had their fun. Let's see what they want to do next."

The piranha bugs, satiated, went home. They went to a strange swamp about fifty-eight kilometres north-west of the *Santa Maria*. Kwango tracked them cautiously, circling the swamp at a distance of about three hundred meters. It was roughly banana-shaped, about two kilometres long and about half a kilometre wide at its widest point. There was not a great deal of vegetation, most of it consisting of tall thick reeds that bowed in the light breeze but also had a curious illusion of motion that had noting to do with air currents. Here and there patches of clear water were visible. From many of them, hummocks rose. On top of each hummock was a whitish, completely symmetrical dome, ridged and looking as if it was made of paper.

Kwango was jubilant. "Piranha Bug City!" he exclaimed. "We hit the jack-pot. This is where those bastards live and breed. Get the vid rolling, baby. Magnification 30. I'll try to keep the chopper steady so you won't get shaky pix."

"Those domes must be their nests or hives," said Mirlena.

"Score one, lovely Expendable. How high would you estimate?"

"Three metres, maybe four. About two metres wide at the base. Can we go in close? I'd like high definition shots."

Kwango shook his head. "Not yet. I don't think those hell-bugs would put out de welcome mat. First, we get all the data we can from a discreet distance. Then I'll take the chopper up and we'll get vertical shots. After that, we'll think again."

"Those reeds," said Mirlena. "They move very strangely. They are blown by the breeze, but they also seem to tipple and they look top-heavy."

Kwango grinned. "Explanation?"

"Not so far. I need to go in closer."

"Score nothing, dearest heart. But not to worry. You are with Kwango. I will give you the key word: larva, chrysalis, imago."

"Of course!" said Mirlena. "It has to be. The piranha bugs deposit their eggs in the water, the larvae crawl up the reeds, pass through the chrysalid stage and become imagos by the time they get to the top."

Kwango nodded. "Dat is why de reeds move funnywise, dear lady. Dey are loaded with young piranha bugs."

"Look!" said Mirlena. "One of the hives is burning. There is smoke coming out of the top."

Kwango gave her a pitying smile. "That smoke is going to resolve itself into a cloud of very hungry bugs, a war party. Let's go topside and take some good shots of Piranha Bug City. The good Commander is going to like this day's work."

He took the chopper up to five hundred metres, centred over the swamp and came down slowly. "Smoke" rose from more than a hundred hives. The air became black with piranha bugs. Kwango lifted hastily.

"Kurt, what the hell are you doing?" demanded Mirlena. "I want to go in low."

"Discretion is the better part of something or other," retorted Kwango. "If those critters got any thinking apparatus, they might just decide to settle all over the chopper. Not only could they blind us by covering the bubble, but they could also bring us down by sheer weight of numbers. We have the data we need. Now is the time to go home."

Phase Seven

The Harpoon Tree

When Tibor Maleter and Gunnar Norstedt had finished building the menagerie, they went hunting. Each used an exo-skeleton and each carried an anagun. They ranged far and wide.

Their first spectacular success was to bring back a couple of two-tonne rhinotypes—one male and one female. It was Gunnar who had noticed the difference. The males each had one large fifty-centimetre horn on the end of the massive nose, and the females had two smaller horns, one behind the other.

The herd was grazing about fifteen kilometres away from the *Santa Maria*. On their first attempt at collecting specimens, the Expendables failed. The bulls saw the exos coming at them while Gunnar and Tibor were nearly two kilometres away. They signalled the rest of the herd, which instantly stampeded.

But five bulls remained to meet the challenge. Gunnar and Tibor moved up slowly. The anaguns felt like tiny toys in their exo-hands, being designed for use by human beings or standard size robots. Which was why the first attempt failed. Before the Expendables could get close enough to use the anaguns accurately, the bulls charged. Tibor had difficulty pressing the small firing stub with his huge exo-fingers without crushing the gun. When he did succeed, his aim was erratic and the bulls just came on. Gunnar got so excited that he crushed the anagun as if it were made of thin plastic.

And still the bulls came on.

They charged at 30 k.p.h. and they aimed for the exo-legs, which were the only part of the metal monsters that the animals could hope to reach.

They connected; and the force of the impact knocked both exos down. It was as if human beings had been hit almost simultaneously on the shin-bones by heavy foot-balls.

As the exos toppled, Gunnar Norstedt uttered several colourful profanities.

One animal had broken its neck on impact, and lay writhing and dying, another had temporarily stunned itself. The three survivors tried to gore and trample the metal giants who had threatened the herd.

Maleter had blacked out briefly as his head hit the harness frame when the exo went down. Gunnar Norstedt suffered only a bruised pride. But by the time they had both recovered their wits, the surviving bulls had realized that they were not having too much effect in their attempts to flatten the alien monsters.

As Norstedt struggled to a sitting position and cautiously put out a massive hand to scoop up one of the rhinotypes, the bulls roared indignantly and retreated at great speed, presumably to rejoin the herd that was now far away, near the horizon.

"You O.K. Tibor, my friend?"

Maleter picked himself up. "I have a bump on the back of my head. I wish I could rub it; but if I do, the exo-hand will probably make a mess of the dome."

"I think you are right," said Norstedt. "I think also we have adopted the wrong technique for catching these jokers. Does your anagun still work? Regretfully, and with some afflatus, I have crushed mine into junk."

Maleter poked about in the grass gently, then found and

picked up the comparatively tiny anagun. He examined it. "Mine works, Gunnar. The trouble is my exo-fingers are too clumsy to operate it."

"Ah, so." Norstedt laughed. "Then we think Kwango."

"Think Kwango?" Maleter was puzzled.

Norstedt got his exo upright. "Ve consider how the maestro would hef got himself a rhino."

Maleter also put his exo upright, and laughed. "You are right, Gunnar. And we know how the black genius would have done it, do we not?"

Norstedt let out a great roar of laughter. "*Ja*, by damn. That Kwango would make the rhinos do the work. Then he would just pick one up like a pussy cat and put it to sleep."

"Let us get after that herd, my friend. We can outrun them, and we can outthink them."

They caught up with the herd very quickly.

The formula was repeated as before—by the rhinos but not by the Expendables.

When the bulls charged, both men waited until the last moment then made their exos leap four metres into the air. The bulls could not stop their charge and went hurtling on. It took them fifty metres to pull up. They made angry noises and turned and charged again. Repeat performance: the exos leaped high. The frustrated bulls gave vent to their anger. And tried again. And lost.

After six or seven passes, they were exhausted. But they were too stupid to know it. They returned to the attack, ambling wearily.

"This time," said Tibor.

"This time for sure, by damn," agreed Gunnar.

They did not jump. They just stooped and gently plucked up two very tired bulls, half-crazed with fear and bewilderment as they were lifted clear of the ground. To the men in the exo-skeletons, the weakly struggling bulls felt like large playful cats.

Maleter very carefully tapped his bull on the head with an exo fist. The bull bellowed indignantly but did not lose consciousness. He hit it again. This time it went limp.

"Hef you killed it?"

"No. It's still breathing, Gunnar."

"Vot force should von applicate, mien komerad?" Norstedt's speech always went to pieces when he was excited.

"I don't know. You have to experiment."

Gunnar hit his bull. It bellowed with pain and rage. He hit it again. It bellowed even louder. Exasperated, Gunnar brought the exo fist down more heavily—and promptly broke the animal's neck.

"Sheet and derision!"

Maleter was perplexed. "What did you say?"

"I say sheet and derision. Iss good Anglo phrase meaning Goddam and by golly gosh. I hef clumsywise made the poor bastard fairly dead." He laid the corpse down gently. "No matter. Who wants two bulls, anyway? I go get a cow. That is good thinking. The bull you got will be pleased, Conrad will be pleased, maybe the goddam cow will be pleased. Stay here my friend. I will return pronto."

The irrepressible Swede was already making his exo run across the grassy plain at 70 k.p.h. before Maleter could reply. His bull woke up and wriggled half-heartedly. He hit it again and it went back to sleep. Diplomatically, he put it on the ground at some distance from its dead brother.

Maleter called Norstedt on the exo-radio. Norstedt's exo was already five kilometres away. "Can you see the herd, Gunnar?"

"*Jawohl*. Iss about three kilometres ahead. Soon I make mit der funnies."

Norstedt did indeed make mit der funnies. Upon his approach, the herd stampeded according to previous ritual, while three bulls remained to face the enemy and charge.

With consummate timing, Norstedt leaped over them at the last moment. Before they had realized what was happening, he was away in pursuit of the herd.

The rhinotypes could not move as fast as a man in an exo-skeleton. Soon he was among them. The beasts panicked and ran off in all directions. But Norstedt managed to snatch up a cow. He hit it very gently, and was grateful to feel it go limp. He checked carefully that it was still breathing.

He called Maleter. "Success, dear friend and brother sadist. The lady is willing. Let us return to base mit der valuable specimens. Monsignor Conrad will be much impressed."

Monsignor Conrad was much impressed. He was at the command screens at the time and was privileged to observe two metallic giants striding across the landscape with what in the distance looked like dead cats in their hands.

He radioed. "Dead or alive?"

Norstedt answered. "Alive, but discommoded, *mon capitaine*. Male and female. Howzat?"

"Not bad," conceded Conrad. "Stick them in separate pens for the time being."

*   *   *

After lunch—Kwango and Mirlena were not present —Norstedt and Maleter harnessed up again and went out in search of more game.

"Let us go up to the hill country," said Norstedt. "It could be that we find quite different types of creatures up there."

"But the hills are more than sixty kilometres away."

"So? You get tired walking in an exo?"

"No, but——"

"If ve see anything good on the way, ve stop and knock it off," said Norstedt. "Zis time I am fully prepared. See! I have plenty sacks for small furry indigenes and other somesuch." He displayed an exo handful of the large plastic bags in which the exo-components had been stored on the *Santa Maria*.

Having harnessed up, the two men left the perimeter. "I hope you have air-holes in those plastic bags," said Tibor. "The commander won't like it if you bring back asphyxiated specimens."

"Listen, sonny," retorted Gunnar with some conviction, "all my specimens will be clean."

It was not long before they encountered several animals

that looked oddly like giant pandas. But unlike the Terran pandas they were very fast. In panic, they darted about randomly but at high speed.

Maleter accidently stepped on one, crushing and killing it instantly. But Norstedt was lucky enough to snatch one up without damage. He held it still while Maleter, fumbling with the tiny anagun, carefully shot a dart into its back. The animal uttered a great—almost human—sigh and went limp.

"How long will it sleep, Tibor?"

"Maybe a couple of hours."

"Good. I will pop it in der bag and pick it up on the way back."

Rather clumsily, he dropped the animal into one of the plastic bags and bound the top tightly with a length of steel wire.

"Are you sure that thing has air-holes in it?"

Gunnar poked an exo-finger twice through the plastic. "It has now, my friend. I will leave our new playmates where it cannot fail to be seen on the way back."

He found a grassy knoll and dumped the bag containing the unconscious animal on top of it.

They proceeded north. *En route* they came across a large flock of the flightless birds that had been sighted in the distance a day or two before.

The birds registered the presence of the exos when they were about a kilometre away. They did not seem too concerned, and continued to graze on the leaves of a patch of shrubs.

But when the exos were about a hundred metres away, the birds stopped grazing and stared stonily at the intruders.

"Now, we hef more specimens for Conrad's zoo," said Norstedt. "I vunder how dose big bastards flavour? *Unser* robots vill have much fun cooking fifty kilos of Argus turkey on Christmas Day."

"Gunnar, your English gets worse and worse," said Tibor. "How do you do it?"

"Iss my secret, friend. I hef much loquacious craft."

The birds had long necks like ostriches and long legs.

111

They were more than two metres tall. And, like ostriches, they had a remarkable turn of speed.

"Let us go in and get two," said Tibor.

But this was one occasion where the exos were outclassed.

As the Expendables approached, the birds gobbled, squawked and finally uttered noises that sounded as if they had been made by king-size demented hunting owls.

They waited until the exos were only ten metres away. Then they moved. Maleter and Norstedt were amazed. The exos could achieve 70 k.p.h. but the wingless birds of Argus could do more than 80 k.p.h. And didn't look as if they were really trying.

At first, the two Expendables refused to believe that their exos could be outpaced by those large clumsy birds which, with their long necks, fluffy blue feathers and disproportionately small heads, looked like animated cartoon creatures—mere travesties of living things.

They gave chase, assuming that the birds were only capable of such a speed in short bursts. They were wrong. After ten kilometres, they knew they were wrong. The ostrich-like creatures had become mobile dots in the middle-distance.

Both men were panting with the effort of simulating running motions while in harness. The exo control domes were air-conditioned; but that did not help too much. The sun was high, and it was a hot day.

They came upon a tree—a solitary tree in the middle of a great stretch of grassland. At least, it looked like a tree since it possessed a central trunk more than thirty metres high and more than three metres in diameter at the base. The curious thing was that it didn't seem to have any branches. Also, the top flattened out like the inverted head of a giant mushroom. Also, there were three smaller, subsidiary trunks fanning out, each with the inverted mushroom head, but clearly attached to the main trunk and, presumably, the roots. Long black tendrils were pressed close to each of the trunks. They rose above the mushroom heads and swayed in the light breeze. At the end of each tendril was what looked like a barbed thorn. Possibly, the strands that grew up the trunks were parasitic, like ivy. Possibly, they were part of the tree itself. Whatever the huge growth provided the only shade available.

"I am hot and sticky," said Tibor. "It was a mistake to try to take a couple of those birds. I am going to unharness and lie flat on my back for a while in the shade of this tree. How about you, Gunnar?"

"I, too, am hot and sticky. Zose goddam birds are a pain in my rectum. I am truly mortified. But the good commander has issued instructions that we are not to expose ourselves. Iss so?"

"Iss so," agreed Tibor, drily. "But there are no piranha bugs around, and we can take precautions. You take fifteen minutes out, while I remain in harness. Then I'll take fifteen minutes out while you remain in harness. We both refresh ourselves. No problem."

"Agreed," said Gunnar. "But you take the first siesta, *mein freund*. I vill sit on my exo-arse and votch over you like a mutter."

Maleter unharnessed and wriggled out of the prone exo with a great sigh of relief. He leaned back on the grassy turf in the shade of the tree, about five metres from its base, and relaxed.

Norstedt made his exo sit down with a ground-shaking thump, and crossed its legs. He looked like a cybernetic Buddha.

"Iss a pleasant day, Tibor—if one does not hef to rush about in zees beer cans with legs on."

Maleter stretched luxuriously. "Yes, it's very pleasant, Gunnar. If we can prove this planet, the colonists should be able to——"

He never finished the sentence.

Suddenly, there was a great whistling in the air, followed by cracks that sounded dully like old-fashioned gunfire. Norstedt was aware of things rattling on his control dome. Something or some things were repeatedly striking the exo all over. He saw only blurred movement. "*Vot der teufel——*"

He looked at where Tibor should have been. But Tibor wasn't there.

Norstedt got his exo upright, ignoring all the rattling and the movement.

He looked round him. Thick black rope-like things were floating all about the exo.

He glanced up.

And saw Tibor Maleter in mid-air.

The Hungarian was transfixed, pierced by a great barbed thorn that had penetrated his chest with such force that its now bloody arrowhead had gone clean through the body. The thorn was on the end of one of the thick cable-like tendrils that only a few moments before had been pressed close to the trunk of the tree.

But now all the long black thorn-headed things were in crazy motion, some striking at the exo, others lashing out at Maleter. It was a fantastic sight. For a moment or two, Norstedt froze in horror. Two more thorns plunged into a still feebly writhing body, while the black tendrils lifted it higher and higher.

Norstedt's wits returned.

Tibor, dripping blood, was already eight or nine metres above the ground, being inexorably drawn higher.

Norstedt ignored the things attacking his exo and put out both hands and gripped the stems that had impaled his companion. Using all his exo-power, he crushed the thick black rubbery things and tore them clean away from the mother tree.

Skilfully, he caught Tibor's body before it could fall.

He took it clear of the tree and laid it gently in the grass. There was no point in trying to get the great thorny stubs out. The Hungarian was already dead.

Norstedt gazed down at the body of his companion with horror. Then his mind began to function.

He used the transceiver. "Mayday! Mayday! Mayday! Come in *Santa Maria*. For der luff of Gott, come in *Santa Maria*!"

Conrad's voice answered. "Tell it quickly, Norstedt. We have a direction fix on you."

"Tibor is dead," babbled the big Swede. "Some bloody great devil tree shust stuck him mit der harpoons—and poof. Poor bastard iss dead."

114

Even as Norstedt spoke, an extra long tendril whistled out from the dreadful tree and transfixed poor Tibor's body yet again. Before Norstedt could move, the dead Expendable was whipped high into the air and dropped neatly and obscurely into the inverted mushroom-like top. The corpse disappeared.

The swollen top of the hideous plant was, in fact, a great gaping mouth—wide enough to accept even the largest rhino.

"God's blood!" Norstedt was appalled. His voice sank to a whisper. "Zet monstrous thing has eaten poor Tibor, by damn."

"What's that?" Conrad's voice rasped over the transceiver. "Pull yourself together, Norstedt. Report your situation. Are you personally safe? Speak up man!"

"Yes, sir." The sharpness of Conrad's voice had the desired effect. "I am in no danger, Commander. I am in my exo. Dis—dis harpoon tree has had a go at me, but it can achieve nothing."

"Wasn't Tibor in his exo?"

"No, Commander."

Conrad let out a great, audible sigh. "When will you people ever learn to obey orders? Now maybe you will realize that Argus is not a garden party."

"Yes, Commander."

"I'm on my way as fast as this bloody hovercar will go. Remain where you are unless you are endangered. I have with me Lieutenant Smith, Matthew and some laser rifles. E.T.A. twenty from now. Improve the shining minutes, Norstedt, by giving me a coherent account of what has happened. Over."

Gunnar Norstedt discovered with some wonderment that the ground was shaking. He realized why. It was shaking because he was shaking and, therefore, the exo was shaking.

Suddenly, he was ashamed. With a great effort of will, he commanded himself not to shake. Amazingly, his body obeyed the command. Then, in atrocious English, he described the entire sequence of events.

Phase Eight

The Hideous Mouth

Conrad stared up at the monstrous growth. On the three worlds the Expendables had proved, he had never seen any plant quite so grotesque or formidable in appearance. The almost tentacular harpoon shoots had now returned to their original positions, pressed close to the main trunk, their barbed tips waving above the mushroom head rhythmically. The main trunk and the subsidiary trunks were green and purple, with an exposed network of what looked like whitish veins.

Inspecting the thing through a monocular at mag ten, Conrad saw that the trunks were smooth and rubbery, almost fungoid.

He had grounded the hovercar at a distance of fifty metres from the plant. He and Lieutenant Smith wore armorlite jackets as well as their protective suits. It would take a harpoon made of tungsten steel to penetrate that combination.

Matthew stood beside the hovercar, imperturbable as always. In his exo, Norstedt towered above them all. Tibor Maleter's exo still lay within range of the deadly harpoons, near the base of the tree.

Conrad used his transceiver. "Well, Norstedt, you and Maleter seem to have hit the jackpot."

Norstedt shrugged, and the eight-metre exo perfectly reproduced his movement—but in subtle parody. "I cannot forgive myself for this thing, Commander. Tibor was my friend. It vos stupid to let him get out of de exo, but ve vos not to know."

"Don't feel guilty," said Conrad, "but remember that you were both stupid. Profit by his death. This game is not for people who get stupid. . . . Now get in there and pull his exo clear. I want to see what happens."

"Yes, Commander."

"What if those harpoon things break through the plexiglass in his control dome?" asked Indira.

"They won't. But if by some miracle they do, Matthew and I will laser that thing to ashes. Get the vid rolling, Lieutenant. I want this sequence on tape . . . Matthew, if Mr. Norstedt appears to be in difficulty, you will laser the base of the plant at maximum power. I will take care of the tendrils or tentacles or whatever they are."

"Decision noted, Commander."

Norstedt took his exo forward. Immediately the harpoon appendages struck at him. There was no damage, only inconvenience. Norstedt dragged Maleter's exo out of range using one exo hand to haul it and one to beat off the striking harpoons.

"Interesting," said Conrad. "I wonder if that thing reacts to movement, to pressure or to both."

"James, how can you be so cold-blooded? Gunnar has just risked his life."

"No problem, Lieutenant," retorted Conrad coldly. "We are all in the business of risking our lives. Don't call me James and did you tape it?"

"Yes—sir."

Norstedt radioed: "Ow vos dat, Commander?"

"Not bad, Gunnar. Were you scared?"

"*Ja, oui* and yes."

"Good. You're learning."

"Commander," said Matthew, "the main section of the plant has begun to move. It is inclining towards us. Estimated rate of movement of circular top section, fifty centimetres per minute."

"I can't see any difference in its attitude," said Conrad.

"Sir, the efficiency of the human eye compared with ——"

"Cancel statement," said Conrad wearily.

"Decision noted. Execution proceeds."

"It *is* moving, James," said Indira. "I can see more of the head. I am sure it is not because of the breeze."

"You are right . . . Sorry, Matthew . . . It is trying to

117

get us in range. Interesting! Perhaps it has sensing mechanisms that correspond to eyes . . . Lieutenant Smith, keep the vid rolling . . . Matthew, take two paces forward."

"Decision noted, sir. Execution proceeds."

The robot stepped two paces forward. As it did so, the massive plant perceptibly quivered and the huge mushroom head that in reality concealed a cavernous orifice, inclined more rapidly. It was as if the whole rubbery trunk or massive stem had a kind of muscular system that enabled it to move deliberately.

"Rate of movement now approximately eighty-five centimetres per minute," commented Matthew.

"Take two more paces forward."

"Decision noted, sir. Execution proceeds."

As Matthew moved, the whole plant seemed to ripple with anticipation or excitement. But that was purely imagination, Conrad told himself. The bloody thing could not have a central nervous system.

A harpoon whipped out at Matthew, and fell short. It recoiled instantly.

"Take two more paces forward, Matthew."

"Decision noted, sir. Execution proceeds."

Now the huge main head of the plant was moving rapidly enough to be perceived by the human eye. The entire trunk was bending. It was as if the huge growth was bending down to inspect the comparatively small creature that had dared to approach it.

Two more harpoons whistled out. They rattled harmlessly off Matthew's chest plate.

Now the hideous head was inclined almost at right-angles to the ground. The inverted mushroom—nearly six metres in diameter—was exposed as a dark, gaping hole. A red-rimmed revolting caricature of a human mouth. Behind the rubbery, fungoid lips were rows of whitish thorn-like protuberances—used, presumably, to keep the prey trapped once it had been dropped into that awful hole. The thorn-like things looked eerily like double rows of fangs.

More harpoons attacked Matthew. He stood still, waiting impassively for Conrad's next command.

Indira was very pale. "This is the most revolting thing we have ever——"

"Worse than the deathworms?" Conrad gave her a thin smile. "Or has time softened the memory?" Before she could reply, he went on: "I am going to harness up and get in there and see what this bloody thing is like."

"James, please——"

"Just keep the vid rolling, Lieutenant. And keep out of range." Expertly, he harnessed up in Tibor's exo-skeleton. He made the exo stand up.

"Listen, Gunnar: this is exactly what we are going to do. That trunk is very flexible as we can see. Judging from the way the thing is bending towards Matthew, it is a bit cross that it can't harpoon him. Now, when I give the word, we are going in fast. Your task is to grip the trunk and bend it still further. My task will be to leap up to that bloody great hole and see what is inside it. O.K.?"

Norstedt's voice was none too steady. "Ef you say so, Commander."

"Are you monitoring this conversation, Lieutenant?"

Indira operated the vid with one hand and her transceiver with the other. She glanced up at Conrad in his control dome. "Yes. James, you are a bloody fool. There is no knowing what——"

"Belay that, Lieutenant . . . Matthew, do you read me?"

"I read you loud and clear, Commander."

"These are my instructions. Upon the word Go, you will move quickly back to the right, out of range, while Mr. Norstedt and I go in. I do not anticipate any problem that cannot be handled by the exos; but if we appear to be in difficulty or call for help, you are to laser at maximum power all the harpoon appendages and then the base of the plant. If either or both of the exos are immobilized, you will not attempt to retrieve them until the plant is totally destroyed. Under no circumstances will you allow Lieutenant Smith to approach the area while any part of this thing still functions. Execute!"

"Decisions noted, Commander." Matthew sounded

slightly aggrieved, as if he resented the implication that he *might* allow Lieutenant Smith to put herself at risk.

"Go!"

Matthew moved with extraordinary speed and agility. So did the exos.

Norstedt put out his exo-hands, dug the long steel fingers right into the plant's rubbery trunk and pulled savagely as if he were determined to snap the massive thing. The plant's responses were amazingly fast. Harpoons began to flail and whip at the exos. It looked as if the plant had already registered, somehow, that it could not penetrate its attackers with a harpoon strike and was therefore trying to beat them to the ground.

Under the fury of Norstedt's assault, the hideous, mouth-like orifice came lower. Now it was only about fifteen metres above ground level. Conrad's eight-metre exo leaped high. The exo hands reached up and gripped the thick, rubbery pseudo-lips, the exo legs clamped round the upper trunk in a vice-like grip.

Conrad hauled himself higher, switched on his headlight and poked his control dome right into the dreadful opening. At first, he saw only a dark fluid slopping about, its surface agitated by Norstedt's efforts and his own.

Then he saw what was left of Tibor Maleter, floating in the fluid which, obviously, was the plant's gastric juice. Tibor's clothes had already been dissolved by the acid. Most of his head was gone, and there was little left of his arms and legs.

Tibor was floating face down—for which Conrad was grateful. The flesh had been mostly dissolved away from the torso. The scapulae and spinal column were exposed. The fluid bubbled around the body and vapour rose from the action of the acid on the already half-dissolved corpse.

Conrad had seen enough. He lowered his exo down the trunk and called Norstedt.

"O.K., let it go, Gunnar. Let's get the hell out."

Norstedt withdrew his exo-fingers from the trunk and was gratified to see that where he had penetrated it, the tree was weeping a dark fluid.

The two exos, still wea ly attacked by the harpoon

appendages, backed away. The tree began to straighten itself.

"What did you find?" called Lieutenant Smith anxiously.

"Nothing much," lied Conrad. "Some fluid, that's all. It was very dark in there."

"No sign of Tibor's body?"

"No sign."

Norstedt said: "Ef it is hokey with you, Commander, I vud like to take zis thing apart mit mein exo-hands."

Conrad had a sudden vision of Norstedt tearing the thing to pieces and causing it to spew out the partially digested remains of Tibor.

"Permission denied," snapped Conrad.

"Iss personal thing, *mon capitaine*. Zet bastard ex-crescence has destroyed my friend. I vud feel better."

"Don't feel better, feel worse. You allowed Maleter to disobey orders . . . And another thing, Norstedt. Improve your English . . . Do you read me, Matthew?"

"I read you loud and clear, sir."

"Laser this tree, Matthew. Maximum burn. Laser the heads first. Burn them good. Then take out the appendages and work down the trunks. When you have done that, laser the roots. I want nothing left here but a crater. Understood?"

"Understood, Commander. Decision noted. Execution proceeds."

"You saw him!" Instinctively, Lieutenant Smith knew why Conrad had given the command for total destruction.

Conrad ignored the comment. "Lieutenant Smith, when Matthew has finished you will take the hovercar back. Norstedt and I will pace you with the exos."

Matthew was efficient. Systematically, he burned the harpoon tree from top to bottom. The hideous heads withered, blackened, smouldered, died, burst into flame. Black smoke rose, billowing. The harpoon tendrils shrivelled, withered, became incandescent. Matthew burned on. Presently there was a crater six metres wide and two metres deep.

"Execution completed, Commander."

"Thank you. Return to the hovercar and take Lieutenant Smith back to the *Santa Maria*. Thirty k.p.h. Execute."

"Decisions noted, sir. Execution proceeds."

Indira said: "James Conrad, I love you. That was Tibor's funeral pyre, wasn't it?"

Conrad gave a grim laugh. "Logically, I should have preserved that monstrosity. Kwango would have wanted to inspect it. But we Expendables dispose of our dead honourably—when we can. Tibor has just been cremated. He was an atheist. He wouldn't have wanted any fine words; but he might have appreciated this little gesture . . . Let's go."

Stage Three

The Sting

Phase One

How About Proving This Bloody Planet?

That evening, in the saloon of the *Santa Maria*, dinner was a very subdued affair. Normally, there was much discussion of the day's events and discoveries. Normally, Conrad asked many questions, keeping his mental "progress chart" up to date. But that evening dinner was a matter of long silences, and much food left on the plates.

All the Expendables were present. Matthew was on watch at the command screens. The robot Mark was in attendance in the saloon.

The Expendables were eating their first meal of Argus food. It should have been a topic for conversation. It wasn't.

Conrad tried to set an example. He ate everything that was put before him. He was the only one who did so.

Finally, Norstedt appeared to come to some kind of decision. "Permission to speak, Commander?"

Conrad ignored him. "Mark, serve brandy. Glasses, six. Point two five litres Hennessy XO equally apportioned. Execute."

"Decision noted. Execution proceeds."

With remarkable speed and efficiency, Mark brought the glasses, poured the brandy.

Norstedt tried again. "Permission to speak, Commander?"

Conrad shrugged. "Permission granted, Gunnar. But you don't need it when we are dining together."

"Zis iss a formal occasion, sir."

"Is it? Why is it? I was not aware of it."

Norstedt was not to be put down. "Iss a formal occasion, Commander, because I vish to make a formal request. It costs nothing. I shust vish to build a monument for my

125

friend Tibor Maleter. I haf some religion—not much, but some . . . I vish to leave der marker, vich I vill construct mit mein own hands."

Conrad gave a faint smile. "Request granted. But you will do it in your own time, Norstedt, not in *my* time. And for the next few days, you won't have any time of your own. Because when you aren't working, you will be resting and sleeping. That is my time, too." He gazed at the rest of the Expendables. "I have revised my strategy for the proving of Argus. But more of that anon . . . Ladies and gentlemen, I ask you to raise your glasses to Tibor Maleter."

"Tibor," said Norstedt, lifting his glass. "I trink to der memory off my good friend. Thank you, *mon capitaine.*"

"Tibor," repeated Maeve and Mirlena. Lieutenant Smith raised her glass, but said nothing. She knew what was coming.

Conrad sipped his brandy and put his glass down. "A man who, by his idiocy in disobeying orders—aided and abetted by our sentimental Swede—managed to put this project at risk. In dying, he reduced our effective manpower by some 15 per cent, which was pretty damn careless of him."

Norstedt slammed his glass down so hard it broke. "Commander, I will not hef my friend——"

"Shut up, Gunnar. Your atrocious accent bores me." He turned to Kwango. "Kurt, what is your opinion of Tibor?"

Kwango shrugged. "A no-good layabout, Boss. He played lousy chess—even lousy for a Hungarian."

"His unarmed combat was not exactly brilliant," said Conrad. "In the training programme, I hit him twice with my bio-arm and he fell apart. While he was on the mat, he should have gone for my legs. He didn't. He just stood up and let me hit him again."

Norstedt was red in the face. He stood up angrily. "Commander, zis is *de trop*, too fucking much. Ef you will step outside zis place, I vill be happy to——"

"Shut up, Gunnar," said Indira fiercely. "You don't know what they are doing."

"Sit down, Norstedt," snapped Conrad. "You are an idiot. If you do not sit, I will first reduce you to Swedish mincemeat and then I will log you for disobeying an order."

Mirlena Robinson flared up. "Commander Conrad, you are outrageous!"

"So I am, Robinson, so I am. And so were you when you went picking blue mushrooms . . . Where was I? Ah, yes, we were discussing Tibor."

"He had a nice nature, Boss," said Kwango. "But he was not so hot in an exo."

"True," agreed Conrad. "Doubtless, he had other sterling qualities. But he did not live long enough to exercise them . . . Well, ladies and gents, the point I am making— I hope—is that Tibor died for nothing. If any more of us die on Argus, let it be for something . . . And if you want to build a monument for him, Norstedt, you can. It will be one million square kilometres of this planet that we have proved safe for colonization.

"Now listen, all of you. Don't get stupid like Mirlena and Tibor did. We almost lost two. We can't afford any more fun and games. This is a killer planet. It doesn't like people. Get the message."

"Talking of people, Boss," said Kwango, "what about my tool-making baboons?"

"We'll come to your tool-making baboons presently, Kurt. As I understand it, the baboons present no immediate threat. Right?"

"Right, Boss. Lieutenant Smith confirms my preliminary findings."

"Good. The baboons will keep, then. The piranha bugs will not. So long as they are around, we are all at risk. And we will take care of whatever harpoon trees remain in our present ten thousand square kilometre block. Fortunately those bastard things are easily recognizable, and we already know how they function. So all we have to do is search the block and burn them. We know nothing about their development cycle, of course. Robinson, would you care to extrapolate?"

Mirlena Robinson stuck out her breasts and gazed at

Conrad coldly. "What kind of extrapolation do you want, Commander?"

Conrad scratched his silver eye-patch. "Use your wits, woman! How long would it take—at maximum speed—for one of those thirty-metre monstrosities to mature?"

"I have no reliable data. Someone stupidly lasered the only specimen so far encountered."

Conrad managed to keep his temper. "Make a guess, Robinson. A good guess, that's all."

"Guessing is not scientific—sir."

"Then be unscientific. That is an order."

Mirlena shrugged. "From what you have told us and from what we have seen on the tape playback, it is a highly complex structure. Therefore, I think its maturation process is probably slow. It 'knew' exactly where to strike, and it 'knew' very quickly. That is interesting."

"I don't want a lecture."

"You are not getting one. You are getting a rough and ready analysis based imaginatively on hearsay and ten minutes of videotape. I suspect it is not light-sensitive and therefore could not 'see' you. No specialized organs are apparent. I do not think it is sound-sensitive. When you and Gunnar were in your exos, you communicated by transceiver." Mirlena gave a faint smile. "It is hard to believe that this plant would be monitoring all channels. Therefore, Commander, I assume that you and Gunnar and poor Tibor trod on its toes, which indicates——"

Conrad was still trying not to lose his temper. "What the devil are you playing at, Robinson? I want to know about its life cycle."

Somehow, Mirlena managed to stick out her breasts insolently a little bit further. "If you can manage to refrain from interrupting, Commander, I will give you the good guess you want. But first you must understand my reasoning . . . As I was saying, you all trod on its toes and——"

"Of course!" exclaimed Kwango. "Pressure sensitive roots!"

Mirlena did not seem to object to Kwango's interruption. "Pressure sensitive roots," she agreed. "There was one main stem or trunk and some subsidiary or immature stems. I infer that propagation is mainly achieved by the extension of king-size rhizomes which, in turn, develop a network of pressure sensitive secondary and tertiary root-threads very near the surface of the soil. This being the case, I would expect the plant you call the harpoon tree to mature at a rate of not less than one metre in height per A-year and probably not more than two metres. Therefore, not less than fifteen years to maturation and not more than thirty."

"Now we are getting sensible," said Conrad with some relief. "So, if we can take out all the harpoon trees we find in the proposed colonization area of one million square kilometres, it will be several years before the potential colonists have to do some more weeding."

Mirlena smiled. "You used a lot of laser energy burning that thing, Commander. It is not necessary. All you have to do is scorch the earth around these things. The pressure sensitive roots will wither and the plants will become 'blind'. They will then starve to death, not knowing where or when to strike."

Conrad said "Thank you, Mirlena."

"My pleasure, Commander."

Conrad turned to Kwango. "Apart from certain nasty things we have discovered, Argus still looks promising. It is about time we had one of the famous Kwango scenarios, Kurt. I want to prove one million square kilometres. Can it be done?"

Kwango nodded. "I think it can be done, Boss. Apart from the piranha bugs, we got a curious set-up here. The animals are herbivorous and some of the vegetation is definitely carnivorous. So far as we know, there are not any omnivores."

"What about your baboons?"

"They are nice and peaceable and they eat fruit. Priority one, in survival terms, is to take out the piranha bugs. The mushroom thing that had a go at Mirlena doesn't matter too much. We have already eliminated it from the primary block. The harpoon trees—we have only encountered one so far—don't present a major threat be-

129

cause they stick out in the landscape. The bugs do, being highly mobile, and definitely not nice."

"We have found only one swamp where the creatures breed and live. Reconnaissance has shown it to be the source of the piranha bugs in the primary block. But since we don't know the range of those things, we must survey all the country within a range, say, of two hundred kilometres. Even using the chopper and hovercar throughout all daylight hours, that will take time. Also, we do not yet have enough data on their habits, metabolism and life cycle. We know their eco-function; but that doesn't help too much."

"And what is their eco-function?"

Kwango grinned. "Obvious Boss. They are game thinners—just like the harpoon tree and the Mirlena mushroom. If there are no animal predators, there have to be alternative ways of thinning out the herds. Otherwise, the herbivores would go on proliferating; just like the dinosaurs did on Terra in de good old days of de carboniferous swamps. Nothing could stop the dinosaurs; so they just ate their environment away and then died. Sad, very sad. Mind you, it took them a hundred and forty million years. But they made it in the end."

Conrad scratched his silver patch. "Kwango you have something up your sleeve."

"Yes, Boss."

"What is it, man? I'm in no mood for funnies."

"Boss, you got an incisive mind. I'm worried about my baboons."

"*Your* baboons?"

"Yes, Boss, *my* baboons. If they can be proved to be people we are wasting our time with the rest of the flora and fauna. Because we will just have to cut the holiday short and go home. Why should we knock ourselves out if, eventually, you have to radio back to Terra and tell them that we have intelligent indigenes here on Argus? Then we'd have to twiddle our thumbs somewhat while U.N. cogitated, and then twiddle 'em some more, waiting for the reply."

Kwango grinned. "So you got two hot potatoes to juggle

130

with, Boss: the piranha bugs and the baboons . . . With respect, I am the only guy here who can find out if the baboons are people."

"I, also, can find out if they are people," said Lieutenant Smith.

"With respect, dear Lady Lieutenant, whom I will love always, you can't. I know your file. You are a passable medico and a very good surgeon. That is all you trained for. Do you know anything about semantics?"

"No, Kurt, but——"

"Do you know anything about socio-cultural evolution?"

"Some. A little."

"A little is not enough, dear Lady. You have observed the baboons longer than I have. But your reports didn't tell me anything I didn't know already. How about politics?"

Indira smiled. "O.K., Kurt, you win."

"Modest as I am," said Kwango, "I must reluctantly point out that I majored in semantics, socio-cultural evolution and political science before I became corrupted by ecology. Q.E.D.?"

"Q.E.D.," agreed Indira. "Must you always go for overkill?"

Before Kwango could reply, Conrad said: "You have made your point, genius. Let's get sensible. How long will it take you to determine the semantic, socio-cultural, political status of those bloody baboons?"

"A good man could do it in forty, maybe fifty days."

"And you, funny man?"

"Maybe ten days, Boss. Hard to say. I have to win their confidence."

"Win their confidence quickly. You have five days. After that, I want to transmit to U.N. If this planet is prohibited, I want to prove another one as soon as possible. The programme is costing Terra a lot of solars and a lot of lives. Remember that."

Kwango shrugged. "O.K., Boss. Five days it is. But I need cover."

"What the devil do you mean by that?"

"It is no good going among those baboons wearing a

suit and a life-support system. I am just not going to make contact that way. They got to see my face, read my expressions, know what I'm like. I need cover from the piranha bugs."

"Right," said Conrad. "Listen everybody. This is the programme. Norstedt, for the next five days, you will take an exo, a laser rifle, an anagun, an armorlite jacket, a suit of life-support system and play mother to Kwango. If any piranha bugs approach the baboon colony, you will laser the cloud instantly. O'Brien and Robinson, I want an in-depth report on the piranha bugs, together with recommendations for rapid and total elimination. You can have the chopper for at least one day, maybe two. I want an accurate count and map of their hives . . . A pity we lost our weapons and explosives man."

"Maeve O'Brien smiled. "You seem to forget I am a chemist, Commander."

"I didn't, Maeve. I know you can give me explosives; but you are not trained in handling them. You don't know about time fuses, remote control detonators, that kind of thing."

"Given time, I could learn."

"Thanks. I'll think about it." Conrad turned to Lieutenant Smith. "You and I get the leg work, Lieutenant. We have to make sure there is nothing nasty in the secondary block. You take the hovercar, I'll use an exo. We can leave the search-and-destroy routine for harpoon trees and what Kwango lovingly calls the Mirlena mushroom to available robots. Matthew should be able to give us four for a limited period. Any questions?"

Kwango pressed his luck. "How about some more of dat lovely firewater?"

Conrad glared at him. "How about proving this bloody planet?"

Phase Two

Kwango Juggles: Indira Runs

Lieutenant Smith grounded the hovercar near a spectacular outcrop of rock. She had never seen anything like it. The outcrop was nearly half a kilometre long and perhaps a hundred metres across at its widest point. It rose steeply out of the ground as if it had been pressed through the surface by some colossal subterranean hand. At its highest point it was perhaps five hundred metres above ground level. From that highest point, every fifty-seven seconds A-time, a steaming fountain of water rose, lasting for eleven seconds and producing transient rainbows in the calm air of the sunny morning.

But the most fascinating thing about the rock formation was its own iridescent colours. The major part of the formation was white and glittering, like polished limestone; but it was also veined with multi-coloured fluorspars, the hues of which changed fascinatingly as the high-pressure fountain pulsed.

Lieutenant Smith was more than seventy kilometres from the *Santa Maria*. It was the second day of her search of the secondary blocks. She had found several harpoon trees and—despite the fact that robots had already been assigned to the task—had given them the treatment recommended by Mirlena Robinson. It would be interesting to see if the horrendous things really did starve to death after their pressure sensitive roots had withered.

She took a personal pleasure in disabling the harpoon trees. She had not known Tibor Maleter well—unlike Norstedt he had been a shy, retiring sort of man—but she had liked him. It gave her some satisfaction to destroy some of the dreadful things that had killed him in such a revolting fashion.

She had also lasered a number of Mirlena mushrooms. That, too, had given her satisfaction. Irrationally, perhaps because of some primeval instinct, she had a special loathing for plants that trapped and ate animals.

Apart from these diversions, her search had so far produced negative results. She had not discovered any more breeding grounds for the piranha bugs. Nor had she discovered any other hostile life-forms. In fact, the search had become a trifle monotonous until she came across this marvelous outcrop. It was truly beautiful. The changing colours of the fluorspars as the fountain gushed were almost hypnotic.

Indira Smith had been working very hard. She felt she owed herself a little time for relaxation. She decided to climb the outcrop and see what it was like on top. Though the surface was steep, there were plenty of footholds. With her atomically powered tin legs, she did not anticipate any difficulty or undue fatigue.

Before she got out of the hovercar, she suited up and put on her visor. Then she checked the vicinity yet again. About a kilometre to the south, a herd of light gazelle-like quadrupeds were grazing placidly. No other animal life-forms were in sight, and the sky was clear of piranha bugs.

Indira got out of the hovercar and approached the outcrop. She would have loved to remove her visor and inhale the good Argus air instead of relying on the bottled stuff. But she was mindful of Conrad's orders: take no chances. Surely there could be no harm in climbing a chunk of rock to see what it was like?

The ascent was easy. The tin legs served her well. There was no trouble until she got up to the geyser. Then the water vapour began to steam up her visor. She wiped the droplets away, and peered about her. There was nothing but multi-coloured rock and the roaring hole from which the hot spring regularly emerged. She decided to go down.

The descent was more difficult than climbing up. Every fifty-seven seconds, the geyser threw up its column of hot water for eleven seconds. Each time she was temporarily blinded.

Each time, she waited patiently for the end of the cycle,

134

and wiped the visor. Even so, she slipped twice and was lucky to regain her foot hold. The third time, she was not so lucky. She fell three metres and lay temporarily stunned on a small ledge. She regained consciousness in a matter of seconds. No bones were broken, but her back hurt. Carefully, she felt herself from coccyx to neck. The suit had been torn, her back had been lacerated. She was not in great pain, and therefore reasonably assumed that the lacerations were not deep.

She continued the descent without much difficulty. Her main worry was how she would explain this little escapade to Conrad. At least, that was her main worry until she got down to ground level.

Then she wiped her vizor again, and saw with horror the cloud of piranha bugs.

*   *   *

Kwango was doing all right. After two days he had made great progress. While Nörstedt remained in the background keeping a vigilant watch for piranha bugs or, indeed, any other kind of threat, Kwango did his best to gain the confidence of the baboons.

Their colony was close to the edge of a forest about thirty-eight kilometres south-west of the *Santa Maria*. They had constructed—as Kwango discovered later—a cluster of elaborate underground homes, each complete with living chamber and sleeping chamber. The walls of the chambers were lined with stones and the floors were covered with *woven* mats.

There were about seventy adult baboons in the tribe and, perhaps, twenty-five infants. They were as curious about Kwango as he was about them.

When he first approached the colony, two or three adult males—presumably on watch—uttered loud sounds that were obviously warning signals. A group of infants that had been playing a catching game with small round stones immediately scuttled for shelter in one of the underground dwellings.

More adults emerged from the underground homes; and

presently a line of them sat or stood facing him impassively. They jabbered to each other, and Kwango discreetly recorded the sounds they made. Apart from operating his recorder, he remained quite still, not wishing to alarm them.

After a time one, more curious and bolder than the rest, cautiously approached him. For a minute or two it stood about a metre away inspecting the strange being that was almost double its own height. Then it plucked up enough courage to come closer. It reached out and touched Kwango's leg. Finally it took hold of his hand, regarded it intently and, apparently, counted the fingers, After which it counted its own fingers. It seemed to derive great pleasure from discovering that it and Kwango had exactly the same number.

It returned to the line and held further conversation. Another adult skilfully climbed up a near-by tree and came down with two fruit which it gave to the adventurous one. The fruit looked like a kind of pear.

Holding the fruit, the adventurous baboon again approached Kwango. It regarded him steadfastly for a moment or two, then offered one of the pears.

Kwango took it. "Thank you," he said.

The baboon sat down, began to peel its own fruit and eat it. Kwango did the same.

This simple act seemed to make all the other baboons relax. They, too, came close to Kwango and some of them began to feel his coverall, his limbs, his shoulders and even his head.

The fruit tasted bitter and its texture was hard; but Kwango ate it stoically and stoically endured all the touching, probing and fingering. From then on, progress was rapid. It was as if the tribe had suddenly decided to accept the stranger.

Even on that first morning, he discovered a great deal. Among other things, he discovered that the tribe had a leader. He had already noticed that one particularly old-looking baboon was frequently consulted by the others and that when the old one uttered, the rest would fall silent. Two females were in constant attendance on the old one. They fed him small fruit, like nuts and grapes, which, presumably, were regarded as a special delicacy, since no other baboon was observed eating them.

Kwango tried to show that he was very interested in the underground apartments. Eventually, he seemed to get the message through and was invited by a series of grunts and gestures from the old one, to go into what seemed to be the largest entrance hole. Since Kwango was almost twice the height of the baboons, he had to crawl on his hand and knees.

The apartments had thatched, liftable roofs which could be propped up by sticks shaped for the purpose. Kwango marvelled at the way the walls were lined with shaped stones and at the neatness of the mats that covered the floor. He wondered why the baboons had constructed such elaborate and partly concealed homes, since there were no animal predators and the climate was pleasantly warm.

There were no animal predators; but there were, of course, the piranha bugs. Kwango concluded that the homes were probably permanent protection against the terrible flying things.

By the end of the first day, Kwango had established a relaxed relationship with the baboons. He had pointed to himself and repeated his own name many times, and he had also tried to imitate some simple baboon sounds—to the general amusement, evidently. Man, it seemed, was not the only laughing animal.

When it came time to return to the *Santa Maria,* Kwango had a hard time convincing the troop that he must leave the forest. The leader, in fact, seemed cross at his departure and jumped about angrily, repeating a harsh loud sound again and again. Kwango shrugged and went on his way. It would have been hopeless trying to get across to them that he intended to return tomorrow.

That evening, after dinner, Kwango depressed Conrad by giving him a summary of the day's discoveries. Then he went to use the ship's computer. He had an idea of the value or meaning of certain sounds he had recorded. He thought the computer might be able to help him extrapolate other meanings. He also spent a great deal of time imitating some of the simpler sounds. It was hard on his throat; but he made progress.

The following day, back at the forest, he began once more the slow exhausting business of establishing communication.

*　　*　　*

Indira realized too late that she had been a fool to climb the outcrop of rock. How many times had Conrad warned everyone not to take chances? She, a veteran Expendable, should have known that she should have concentrated on her assigned task.

The cloud of bugs was a large one. It hung lazily above the hovercar at an altitude of about fifty metres as if trying to make up its collective mind what the strange thing was.

Indira thought rapidly. If she could get to the car and get inside it, she would be all right. But she had grounded the vehicle more than a hundred metres from the outcrop. Kwango had told her that the bugs were fast, and she believed him. With the speed available because of her prosthetic legs, she thought she just might make it to the car. But the door was closed, and she would lose a valuable two or three seconds opening it and getting inside. She did not care to dwell on what would happen if only a few of the dreadful things managed to get into the hovercar with her.

The problem was: was it better to take a chance, stay quite still and sweat it out, or call the *Santa Maria* and report her plight? She had her suit transceiver with her. But even if she called the *Santa Maria*, how long would it take to get help? Mirlena and Maeve had the chopper; and they were more than a hundred kilometres away. Conrad, she knew, was using an exo; but she had no means of knowing where he was.

The piranha bugs didn't seem inclined to move. She willed them to go away, but they wouldn't. That malevolent black cloud had an air of brooding about it—as if it knew that there was prey in the vicinity, but it wasn't yet sure where. A decision was needed quickly.

Indira was standing about three metres away from the base of the rock. Even if she remained motionless, the piranha bugs would soon register her presence. She waited for a few more precious seconds, again willing the dreadful things to go away. They didn't. It was as if they knew, uncannily, that the inert object below them was associated with a living, vulnerable being.

Indira Smith made her decision. Slowly, surreptitiously, so that the movement would not attract any attention, she reached for her pocket transceiver. As she did so, she noticed that her suit glove had blood on it. So not only had the back of her suit had been ripped open by the rock, but the wounds on her shoulders and waist had been bleeding quite heavily. She hoped the piranha bugs had no olfactory sense. Otherwise, she was as good as dead.

"Mayday! Mayday!" Indira kept her voice low in case the wretched things could register sound. "*Santa Maria*, do you read me?"

"I read you." It was Matthew's imperturbable voice. "I have a d/f fix, Lieutenant. What is your status? Are you in danger?"

"Am I in danger?" Indira laughed shrilly. "You bet I am in danger, Matthew. I am outside the hovercar, injured, a hundred metres away from it. And there is a cloud of piranha bugs hovering over the vehicle. Hook me in to Commander Conrad fast."

"Decision noted. Execution proceeds."

There was time lapse of several seconds. Indira gazed anxiously at the cloud of piranha bugs. It was drifting almost indolently towards her. Somehow the bastard creatures had registered her presence.

Then Conrad's voice came in. "Lieutenant, I have the message and I have a fix on you. A rough estimate shows that I am about fifty-four kilometres away. That is about forty minutes travelling in overdrive. Define your situation."

The cloud of piranha bugs moved slowly, as if it wished to make the entertainment last as long as possible.

"It's no use, James," said Indira. "I've had it. Those

dreadful things have registered my presence. My suit has been torn and I'm bleeding. They're coming in for the kill. Remember that I loved you."

"Are your tin legs damaged?"

"No."

Conrad's voice was harsh. "Then use them, you stupid brown bitch! Don't wait for the fun. Go! Go! Go!"

"I'll try."

"Don't try. Do it. And make noises into the transceiver about every five minutes so I'll know where you are heading. That is an order, Lieutenant. Execute!"

"Ay, ay, sir."

Indira pulled herself together and started to run south. The piranha bugs knew they had found what they were looking for. A black, whirling torus came down from the sky and fenced her in.

The piranha bugs had invited themselves to the party.

Indira stopped in her tracks, petrified.

*   *   *

Kwango was making more rapid progress than he would have thought possible. He had found that he could reproduce some of the baboon sounds well enough to be understood. He discovered also that each male baboon had an identity-sound, corresponding in human terms to a name. But the same identity sound applied to all adult females, and yet another identity sound applied to all immature baboons of either sex. Kwango wondered idly if there was a naming ceremony when young adult males became mature and, if so, how maturity was defined.

During the course of the morning, Kwango was offered many delicacies to nibble. He accepted them all, made signs of pleasure, such as he had seen the baboons make, and ate the fruit, praying that none of it would be lethal. Some of the fruit tasted dreadful, some intriguing, some quite pleasant. He managed to dispose of it all with baboon-like signs of satisfaction. That old Kwango charm was beginning to have an effect.

Too much so. A female baboon sidled up to him and presented herself.

For the first time in his adult life, Kwango was utterly nonplussed.

All chatter stopped. The baboons gathered round to watch. Mating, evidently, was a matter of public interest in this little community.

The female's bottom began to change colour. It changed from brown to orange to bright red. She was in a state of high excitation. Fluid dripped from her vagina.

The dreadful silence continued. The baboons expected Kwango to serve the willing and doubtless desirable lady. Sweat dripped from his forehead. He was in one hell of a fix.

Suddenly he had an inspiration. Nearby was a small pile of orange-type fruit. He grabbed three of them and began to juggle. Using both hands, he kept the three oranges going up into the air. The baboons were amazed.

For a few moments, they stared at Kwango solemnly. Then they began to utter sounds that could only be interpreted as laughter. One baboon took three of the orange-like fruit and tried to emulate Kwango. He did not succeed. The oranges all tumbled on his head.

The baboons fell about, laughing themselves silly. Meanwhile, the lady on heat held herself in the mating position and waited patiently.

Finally, a young male baboon realized that Kwango was not going to take advantage of the favour offered. He availed himself of it.

Kwango glanced at the operation with a comic look of amazement on his face. The three orange-like fruit fell on his head.

Apart from the mating couple, who took no notice, the rest of the baboons watched Kwango watching the coupling ritual with rapt attention and three orange fruit at his feet. Their strange grunting laughter became louder and louder. They scratched their heads, hit their chests, broke wind, rolled about. They went hysterical. Tears oozed from their eyes.

The mating baboons paid no attention to the rumpus

or to Kwango. They were doing strange things to each other. Kwango watched, fascinated. It looked as if the two baboons had seen every blue movie that had ever been made. Finally they fell apart, exhausted. When they got their breath back, they, too, began to jabber and laugh at Kwango.

Kwango did not sense any malice in the tribe's reactions to his recent behaviour. He sensed only uncontrollable amusement and affection. He realized that he had just been totally accepted and integrated into their society.

As the village idiot.

* * *

Indira gazed at the whirling ring of piranha bugs surrounding her and knew that within seconds they would begin to play their sadistic games before they came in for the kill.

She could feel the wetness running down her back, the wetness of blood. She wondered again if the piranha bugs had any sense of smell that could lead them to strike at the exposed flesh.

Conrad's voice came from the transceiver. "Indira, are you all right?"

"I—I'm fenced in James. You know how they operate."

"Yes, I know. And you know what to do. *Get moving!*"

She did not trust herself to answer.

"*I said: get moving, Lieutenant!*" Conrad's voice was insulting, patronizing, contemptuous. "Did those freedom fighters in South America fuck your mind stupid as well as your body? *Get moving, Lieutenant.*"

"Ay, ay, sir." The response was automatic. Suddenly, Indira was filled with immense fury. Adrenalin surged. She hated Conrad. She hated the piranha bugs. But she hated Conrad more. She hated him for those filthy disgusting words. Briefly, she remembered Applecross, and the way she had given herself. She wanted to kill Conrad for his stony indifference to her feelings. He knew she was about to die; and all he could do was remind her of the

142

worst thing that had ever happened to her.

Black rage enveloped her. "I'll get you for that, Conrad, you bastard! I'll kick your balls through your skull!"

"I've had better than you in cheap Terran brothels," taunted Conrad.

With a great cry of rage, Indira ran at the whirling torus of piranha bugs. The dreadful things had experienced this act of desperation before. Many times. They were programmed for it. They knew exactly what to do.

Except that, this time, they were not dealing with a half-crazed rhino bull. They were dealing with a Terran woman who had atomically powered prosthetic legs.

As the piranha bugs concentrated to stop Indira, she leaped high. She leaped six metres into the air, well clear of the lethal ring. And then she ran. Instinctively, she ran south. Thirty kilometres an hour, forty kilometres an hour, fifty, sixty, seventy, plus. Indira went into overdrive. The tin legs did not falter. The vizor was beginning to cloud over as she panted. With one hand she flipped it off and threw it away. She could not run far with it on. And if she couldn't run far she was dead, anyway.

The piranha bugs were quick to react. The torus regrouped into a cloud. The cloud had no intention of losing its prey and its fun. It, too, went into overdrive.

Indira clutched the transceiver in her hand like a talisman. She heard Conrad's voice against the wind. "Are you clear, Lieutenant?"

"I'm clear, bastard," she panted. "And I'm coming to get you."

"Good," he laughed. "That should be interesting. I have a fix. We are on a collision course. Matthew has an open channel on us. He now estimates rendezvous in about seventeen minutes. Keep coming, sweetie. I've handled better tits than yours on four Terran continents. You're no problem."

Indira increased speed. She glanced behind her. The cloud of piranha bugs was about four hundred metres away, but it was gaining.

Glancing behind her was a mistake. She fell into a gully. By the time she had picked herself up, several precious seconds had been lost and the piranha bugs had gained about two hundred metres.

Conrad's voice again. "You still with us, Lieutenant?"

Her ribs ached, her throat ached, her arms ached, and she did not want to think about her back.

But she could still make noises—just about. "I . . . I'm not . . . not dead yet."

"Matthew is tracking you," said Conrad, coldly. "He tells me you are ambling along. He says you have been stopping to pick daisies. Those tin legs of yours are not so hot, after all. I seem to recall they even rattle when I lay you."

"You . . . you scum! I'll . . . I'll . . ." She just ran out of words.

Tears were streaming down her face. There was a pounding inside her head. The landscape wavered and darkened a little. She did not care about the pain any more. It wouldn't last too long now.

There was a steep rise about two kilometres ahead. The hill didn't matter. The tin legs would cope with it if she could. But she knew she couldn't. Maybe she was good for another kilometre or so. Maybe not. The landscape wavered and darkened again. She fell down, but somehow picked herself up and didn't waste time looking back.

Conrad cut in again. "We are still on collision course. Give it all you have got, you stupid frigid bitch. Stop idling about! You've gone soft."

"Bastard!" she screamed. "Bastard! Bastard!"

But Conrad didn't hear her. She had just dropped the transceiver. She didn't know it.

The hill was now only a kilometre ahead. She willed herself to make it. Irrationally, she thought it would be better to die on a hill.

The pounding in her head was like thunder. Her arms hung slackly. Her vision was clouding. But, miraculously, the tin legs still obeyed her brain.

"Run!" she willed them. "Run! Run!"

It was, she thought vaguely, another first—the first time in human history that a half-conscious woman was running four times as fast as the best Olympic Gold. What the hell!

Then she saw Conrad's exo.

It came over the top of the hill in great bounding strides. It was heading straight for her.

She managed another half kilometre, laughing and crying and groaning and screaming. Then she fell apart. Her lungs and heart and spirit just could not take it any more. The magic legs slowed down. She wavered drunkenly and fell on her face.

Conrad took a fantastic leap right over her body—a forty metres leap that smashed the exo at ninety k.p.h. with deadly accuracy right into the pursuing cloud. The sound of piranha bugs being crushed on impact with the exo was like a hundred decibel hail storm.

They fell in their thousands. Conrad whirled round and glanced back at Indira's unconscious body. None of the bugs had got to her so far. Maybe they were still trying to figure out what had hit them.

Conrad flailed out with his exo arms. The great metal arms and hands whistled through the air, sliced into the black cloud, became massive and deadly instruments of destruction.

The ground at Conrad's exo-feet was covered deep with smashed, injured or stunned piranha bugs. As his arms flailed he jumped up and down, deriving savage pleasure as each huge exo-foot stamped hundreds of piranha bugs literally into the soil.

If the bugs had a group mind, the group mind rapidly realized when it had had enough.

The cloud—what was left of it—rose hastily above Conrad's exo dome, as if it were contemplating what to do about this latest complication. It stabilized about ten metres above his exo.

Conrad did not give it time for thought. He crouched and then made for the first time an exo-jump that would have put Kwango's best performance to shame.

The exo rose like a guided missile and smashed yet again into the piranha bugs. More sounds like a hundred decibel hail storm. Conrad flailed his arms about for good measure, and took a few more thousand of the creatures out before he hit dirtside once again.

The piranha bugs—the survivors—didn't want to know any more. Hitherto, they had been lords of the planet, driving all living things in fear before them, settling upon their victims, tormenting them at will and then eating them to the bone.

But here was something new. Something they couldn't touch. Something that could strike back with terrible speed and create havoc.

They didn't want to know.

The cloud rose high and zoomed hastily away to the north.

Phase Three

Command Decisions

The chopper was on its way. Mirlena Robinson had already dumped Maeve O'Brien at the abandoned hovercar. Matthew had given them the bearing. And now the chopper was heading south to lift Lieutenant Smith back to the *Santa Maria.*

For two or three minutes, Conrad stamped around savagely on the carpet of piranha bugs. This was something personal. Not one of the bastards was going to be left alive.

When he had satisfied himself that vengeance was complete, he went back to Indira, made the exo lie down, unharnessed, grabbed the control dome's medikit and got out of the machine.

Lieutenant Smith was returning to consciousness. There was blood on her face—she had gashed herself on the first tumble and had not known it—and blood on her coverall. Her white hair was all to hell, and her dirty face was stained with blood and sweat and tears.

To Conrad she looked entirely beautiful.

She sat up shakily, gazed at him in wonder. She knew she ought to be dead.

"James, what happened—a miracle?"

He knelt by her and gently stroked the white hair. "Two miracles, love. You and me." He took the brandy from the medikit. "Drink some of this, stupid. The chopper is on its way to lift you out."

"But how did you stop those dreadful things? They were almost on top of me."

"Drink the brandy."

She drank, coughing a little.

"Kwango would have been proud of my exo style," said Conrad. "I had a ball." He gestured towards the mass of black putrescence. Vapour still rose from the mass of squashed piranha bugs. Indira shuddered.

Then she remembered, forgot her injuries and her fatigue, sat bolt upright. "All those dreadful things you said——"

Conrad kissed her. "Shush, little one. You were petrified. I had to get you going." He grinned. "Hell hath no fury like a woman scorned . . . I wonder who said that?"

"You didn't mean them?"

"No."

"Any of them?"

"No, love." He smiled grimly. "It was a command decision. Could have gone wrong. Could have made you sit down and cry and become piranha bug meat. It was a gamble. I gambled on your pride . . . A command decision . . . Some day, if you are very unlucky, you will know what it's like to have to make such decisions"

Indira put her arms round his neck. "James Conrad, you are one hell of a bastard, one hell of a man. I love you."

The chopper came in low from the north, circled Conrad and Lieutenant Smith, hit dirt at a discreet distance.

Mirlena got out, and came running.

"Is she all right, Commander?"

"She'll live," he said laconically.

He lifted Indira in his arms and stood up. "Let's get her comfortable in the chopper, Robinson. Has O'Brien retrieved the car?"

"Yes, Commander."

147

"Good. Get Lieutenant Smith to the sick bay, soonest. *En route*, alert Matthew to the situation. Tell him I'm strolling back."

"Yes, Commander . . . How the hell did you save her?"

Conrad eased Indira gently into the passenger seat, then turned towards Mirlena. "A touch of male chauvinism, Robinson. That was all that was needed. It comes in useful now and then."

Mirlena was mystified. "If you say so."

"Incidentally, Lieutenant Smith," said Conrad, "for gross carelessness and dereliction of duty, you are fined one booze ration. Until further notice, Mr. Kwango will assume your responsibilities as second-in-command."

"James Conrad, you really are a bastard," said Indira. But her eyes said: I love you .

"Lieutenant," retorted Conrad, "you are fined one further booze ration and your incivility, in the presence of another Expendable, will be noted in the log . . . Lift off, Robinson."

Mirlena took the chopper up very quickly, hoping to blow Conrad off his feet. She didn't succeed. He had anticipated her effort and braced himself.

"That man is quite insufferable," said Mirlena.

"That man," said Indira, happily, "is one hell of a bastard, one hell of a man."

*　　　*　　　*

Lieutenant Smith needed cleaning and stitching. She was lucky. The back wounds were only flesh wounds. No bones or vital organs had been damaged. But two of the gashes were quite deep, and she had lost a fair amount of blood.

Matthew cleaned the wounds, squirted them with an aerosol anaesthetic, then stitched the lips together expertly and squirted aerosol synthaskin over his handiwork. Matthew had full medical and surgical programmes stored in his memory banks.

Lieutenant Smith, lying on her belly, was quite relaxed while he worked. She didn't feel a thing. Conrad, watching

148

the operation, needed a large brandy. Mark brought it to him.

Finally, Matthew hooked up a drip-feed of one half-litre of plasma.

"It is recommended, Commander, that Lieutenant Smith does not resume duty for two full days. It is further recommended that she accepts light meals rich in protein, and liquid nourishment rich in iron. Rest is essential. Tranquillizers may be used."

Lieutenant Smith was indignant. "Look here, I am the doctor in this outfit. I am quite capable of assessing my own condition. I will not——"

"Recommendations accepted, Matthew. Prepare a dietary schedule. Inform me if Lieutenant Smith does not fully cooperate." Conrad, having downed the brandy, now seemed to be enjoying the situation.

"For once, you are on the receiving end, Lieutenant," he said. "I have long waited for this moment . . . Something about poetic justice, I think. Anyway, you will stay here in the sick bay until I and/or Matthew decree otherwise. That is an order."

Lieutenant Smith sighed. "You are a bastard, James."

Conrad laughed. "Lieutenant, you are not doing too well. That little bit of insubordination will cost you another booze ration."

Matthew said: "Decisions noted, Commander. Execution proceeds."

*   *   *

That evening, at dinner in the saloon, Conrad reviewed the situation.

"So now we are temporarily down to five. With luck, Lieutenant Smith will be operational soon, but probably only for light duty. That is the debit side. On the credit side, we have established beyond any reasonable doubt that there are no more breeding grounds for the piranha bugs in the secondary block. Also, if Robinson's assessment of the harpoon trees is correct, an entire generation is now going to be starved to death, having been deprived

149

of its means of sensing prey.

"The problem of whether Kwango's baboons are or are not people remains. They have—so he reports—rudimentary technology, rudimentary language, rudimentary society. One alarming sign of their potential intelligence is that they seem to have accepted him as a kind of village idiot."

"That is unkind, Boss," protested Kwango, "and not very nice. You know the situation I was in. What could I do?"

Conrad smiled. "I will leave that to your imagination . . . Anyway, let me have your report the day after tomorrow. And, Kwango, greatness has just been thrust upon you. When I have finished my meal, I am leaving the compound in an exo and with two robots. At that point, you will assume full command of this mission until my return. If I do not return, you will relinquish command to Lieutenant Smith when you are satisfied that she is fit for duty. You will continue to advise her on all matters concerning future operations. Understood?"

"Understood, Commander." Kwango was amazed. "Boss, just what the hell are you going to do?"

"Take out the piranha bugs."

Everyone gazed at him as if he had gone mad.

"Commander," said Maeve O'Brien. "We have given you a map of the breeding ground, and a résumé of the piranha bug's habits. We know its life-cycle but we do not yet have enough knowledge to be able to synthesize a poison that will act quickly, efficiently and with zero failure rate. The bugs react to light, heat and movement. Unless they can be totally destroyed it is quite possible that survivors could establish another colony in some suitable environment."

"Thanks, O'Brien. I have read your report. You and Robinson have done good work. But I have had quite enough of those blasted things. They are interfering with the mission and providing an unacceptable hazard. I am going to take them out tonight."

"There are one hundred and nineteen hives in that swamp," said Mirlena Robinson.

"Yes, I know. I have your map. I hope it is accurate."

"You can't possibly destroy them all, Commander."

"I can and will."

"Even if you could eliminate the hives," said Maeve, "there still remains the problem of the larvae in the swamp water. They will mature, and the whole sequence will start again."

"You know anything about salmon poaching in the late twentieth century?" asked Conrad.

"No." Maeve was mystified.

Conrad smiled. "You have not yet been able to give me a guaranteed poison. I don't want to wait any longer. So I am going salmon poaching."

"By damn!" said Norstedt. "I know something about salmon poaching, *mon capitaine*. I will come vith you, no?"

"No," said Conrad emphatically. "You will remain here under Mr. Kwango's command."

"Boss," said Kwango, "I wish to ask one little, tiny favour. I think I know what you are going to do. Please do not go kami-kaze and do it the hard way. De good Lieutenant will stamp me into de ground for agricultural fertilizer if she discovers I let you get yourself messed up."

"The good Lieutenant will not be told of this operation till tomorrow," retorted Conrad drily. "At the moment, she is under a cloud, you recall." He grinned. "She is also under sedation. I had Matthew spike her drink. She will be out cold for at least twelve hours. Enjoy your moment of power, Kurt. From the time I go dirtside, you are in absolute command."

Mirlena Robinson stuck out her breasts—insolently. "Commander, you enjoin us all to caution yet you, yourself, are planning a potentially suicidal operation. That swamp is treacherous, the piranha bugs are lethal. If you would have the patience to wait for a detailed scientific programme for their extermination, it would——"

"Shut up, Robinson," said Conrad brutally. "I don't have time to argue with academics. Also I don't have time for your scholarly evaluation. Your track record is not too good. You almost got yourself killed. Remember? I have two things you don't have. I have professional experience as a survivor, and I have this." He tapped his silver eye-patch. "With my infra-red vision and the robot's discrete radar systems, we'll manage . . . Any more questions?"

"Yes, Commander." It was Maeve O'Brien speaking. "Just how do you propose to eliminate one hundred and nineteen hives and all the larvae in millions of litres of swamp water?"

Matthew's voice came over the intercom. "Commander, required equipment has been assembled in the air-lock. Mark and I are ready to go dirtside."

"Has the equipment been checked?"

Matthew's robotic voice sounded reproachful. "Sir, your instructions were followed."

"Good. Transfer it and yourselves dirtside."

"Decision noted. Execution proceeds."

Conrad turned to Maeve. "An interesting question, O'Brien. I haven't got time to answer it. Ask the village idiot. He will know."

Norstedt looked confused. "Who, pliss, is der village idiot?"

"Your temporary commander, Gunnar. He is the village idiot . . . Good night, all."

Phase Four

Kami-Kaze—Yet Again

Conrad did not change his eye-patch over until he hit dirtside. Now that his bio-eye was covered, his brain took several moments to adjust to the different data supplied by the infra-red eye. It always took time to adjust. He was getting better at controlling his immediate reactions; but, oddly, he always felt a slight nausea.

The night was dark, but Conrad no longer perceived light or darkness. "Darkness" now for him was a total absence of heat: "light" came from where heat was being generated.

He looked at his own hands. They glowed in an almost ghostly fashion. He looked at the ground. It, too, glowed patchily where grass still grew. Where the grass had been worn away by the massive footprints of exo-skeletons, the ground was darker.

The entire rising column of the *Santa Maria* glowed. It was bright with the heat dissipating from its life-support systems. But it was brightest of all at the engine-room level, where the radiation shields and the cooling systems had to contain the fierce energy of nuclear fuel.

Matthew and Mark were waiting and ready.

Matthew said: "The thirty seismic charges have been armed. Each charge is set to detonate exactly six hours, seventy minutes, thirty-five seconds from now. The charges have all been placed in the steel wire skip fabricated by Luke according to your specifications. Mark and I have fully charged laser rifles, as you requested. Your exo-skeleton has been serviced and checked. All power systems are at optimum efficiency."

Conrad glanced at Matthew. He saw a dim outline of the robot. He also saw the brighter but hazy network of control circuitry, and the radiance that emanated from the robot's shielded power source.

"O.K., Matthew. I'll harness up."

Conrad walked unerringly to the exo-skeleton. He could see its heat loss and the accompanying halo just as well as he could see the robots. The exo's power source glowed brightly. Its controls systems were duller, but definable.

As Conrad harnessed up, he congratulated himself that, for once, he had beaten Kwango to the draw. Using poor Tibor's seismic charges had been an inspiration.

It was true that Maeve O'Brien had offered to make explosives. But explosives was not her field. She had not specialized, as Tibor had.

Each of the thirty seismic charges consisted of four kilos of solidified nitro-glycerine in a shock-proof, water-proof canister with dual radio and time control systems. Tibor had intended to use them to create artificial earthquakes for geological survey in search of fossil fuels.

Now they had a more important use.

"Rest well, Tibor," said Conrad as he made his exo stand erect. "I'm sure you would approve of the use of your toys."

"Query, Commander," said Matthew. "Please define relevance of statement."

Conrad had forgotten that he had an open channel with the robots.

"Cancel statement. It has no relevance."

"Decision noted. Execution proceeds."

Conrad lifted the skip of seismic charges and placed it on his exo shoulder.

"Let's go. What is your maximum speed, Matthew?"

"Approximately 45 k.p.h., sir, if the terrain is smooth."

"The terrain is smooth," said Conrad. "But watch out for the occasional pothole."

"Commander," said Matthew, with a faint robotic note of disapproval, "we are not programmed to err."

Conrad laughed. "To err is human, to be fully programmed is very useful. Keep it that way."

He made his exo stride out of the perimeter at 50 k.p.h., leaving the robots to track him by radar.

Later, he relented and let them catch him up. The three of them arrived at the swamp in one hour fourteen minutes A-time. Which wasn't bad.

There was heavy cloud, the night was black. But darkness now meant nothing to Conrad. He could see the hives, glowing, pulsating with the body heat of thousands of piranha bugs. One hundred and nineteen hives.

"You know what to do, Matthew. You and Mark will wait until I have partly accomplished my mission. Then you will begin dumping the seismic charges according to the pattern given. If I come unstuck, you will dump the charges anyway. Then you will inform Mr. Kwango of my inability to rendezvous."

"Query, sir. Please define the phrase: if I come unstuck."

Conrad lowered the skip of seismic charges—gently. "If I come unstuck means if I fail to function according to plan."

Slowly, Conrad waded into the swamp. He had studied the map well, and knew exactly where to enter. It was unlikely that any part of the swamp was more than three or four metres deep. Most of it, judging from telephoto evidence and echo-sounding profiles was less than a metre in depth. But even if there were any pockets that were more than eight metres deep—the height of a vertical exo—Conrad was confident that he could survive. The exo-dome was air-tight, water-tight, able to withstand an external pressure of ten E-atmospheres. It had its own life-support system and could, if necessary, give Conrad enough air for sixty hours.

The major problem was not drowning or sinking: the major problem was how to take out each hive without disturbing any of the others. The sixty-four thousand solar question was: were the piranha bugs sensitive to vibration? Well, now he would find out.

Conrad's own theory was that once the creatures had settled for the night in their hives, they became torpid like many hive insects on Terra. If the theory was wrong the operation would be a failure.

The theory was not wrong.

Conrad waded cautiously to the first hummock at the end of the banana-shaped swamp. The mud sucked noisily at his exo-feet as he moved. He eased his way out of the swamp and came on to relatively firm ground. Now he was only a few metres from the shimmering hive. Still no movement. It continued to glow eerily with the heat of the thousands of small torpid killers inside.

"The hives must be made of paper," said Conrad aloud, forgetting about his open channel with the robots. "Those black bastards would need something light to allow all the energy they gain from eating meat to dissipate."

"Query, Commander." It was Matthew's voice. "Is the data significant?"

"Cancel statement. I was talking to myself."

"Decision noted. Execution proceeds."

"What the hell?" thought Conrad. "Let's get the show on the road."

He abandoned caution, and took one giant step forward. He put his exo-feet together and made sure that he was on firm ground. He assessed the dimensions of the hive: two point five metres high, one point five in diameter at base.

"Hole in one," thought Conrad crazily. He leaped high, keeping both exo-feet together. They came down on top of the hive like twin king-size pile drivers. The hive and its dreadful contents were crushed.

Conrad stepped back and looked at the dully glowing excrescence at his feet. Warm vapours rose from it. In infra-red vision, it looked as if he had just started a fire. Several bright points shot up from it like sparks. And, like sparks, they fell or were extinguished. The piranha bugs, evidently, could not operate nocturnally, anyway. Conrad was jubilant.

Back into the swamp. On to the next hummock. The same treatment. The same result. One or two survivors tried to get clear of the carnage. But, as before, the sparks faded and died.

On to the next and the next and the next. The treatment as before. The results as before. Slowly, methodically, Piranha Bug City was being stamped into the ground.

Occasionally, the swamp water came as high as the exo-dome. Occasionally Conrad's exo floundered in the soft mud. Once he fell over and the exo was completely submerged. But he kept his wits, got the machine to its feet and plodded on.

He developed new techniques as he went along. He learned to move quickly through the swamp before the exo-feet could sink too far into the mud. Some of the small hives he smashed with a single blow of his exo-hand. But, mostly, he annihilated the bugs by stamping or jumping.

For a time, he went a little crazy, remembering how near the horrendous creatures had been to destroying Indira. But, even while he was enjoying the orgy of destruction, there was a thin cold element of reason at the back of his mind. It counted the hives destroyed. It assessed strategy.

"Matthew, I have cleared the northern part of the swamp. You and Mark can start placing the seismic charges there. Follow my progress. Your radar scan is efficient?"

"Decision noted, Commander. Radar scan is efficient. Execution proceeds. You now have one hour, nineteen minutes, twenty seven seconds before the seismic charges detonate."

"It is enough."

"According to current scan, there are still thirty seven hives to be eliminated, sir."

"Correct."

"Shall I re-time the detonators, sir, to allow for a margin of error?"

"No, Matthew. Proceed as instructed."

"Decision noted. Execution proceeds."

That was Conrad's mistake. He had become too confident.

The trouble did not come until there were only three hives left, grouped close together near the southern tip of the banana-shaped swamp.

Conrad had experienced a little difficulty with some of the larger hives in the central area of the swamp. They had proved too large to smash in one go. Experimentally, he had tried lifting one of the larger hives to drop it in the swamp water. The thing was very fragile and crumbled in his exo-hands.

In infra-red vision, it was like an old-fashioned firework exploding. The piranha bugs, aroused from their torpidity, fountained upwards like a myriad glowing sparks. For a moment or two, Conrad thought he had ruined the operation, and that the survivors might take off from the area of destruction to found another colony elsewhere. But the sparks did not rise more than ten or twelve metres. Then they began to pale and fall down. Most of them were extinguished before they hit the swamp water.

"Curious metabolism," said Conrad. "The bastards need their hives to dissipate their collective heat. But if they

157

are exposed to the night air, the individual heat loss becomes fatal. That will be something to amuse that black bitch with the big tits."

"Query, sir," said Matthew. "Are you still talking to yourself?"

"Yes, Matthew. Cancel statements. This operation is beginning to look like taking candy from babies. Cancel that statement also. And follow me close with the seismic charges. The entire mission should be finished in less than half an hour."

"Decisions noted. Execution proceeds."

Conrad worked his way through the rest of the swamp with great speed. He stamped on the smaller hives, jumped on the medium-sized one and took the largest ones apart with his exo-hands. He no longer worried about the bugs that escaped. They simply rose and died because of rapid heat loss.

He waded towards the last three hummocks.

"How many seismic charges are left, Matthew?"

"Two, sir. Mark has one and I have one. We will deposit them in the required positions after you have eliminated the remaining hives. The time margin is now thirteen minutes, eleven seconds."

"Dump the charges now. It will only take me five minutes to dispose of the last three hives. Then we can all sit back and enjoy the party."

"Decision noted. Execution proceeds."

Mark lobbed the seismic charge so that it hit the swamp water three metres behind Conrad's exo-skeleton. Matthew tossed his ahead of the exo, close to the hummocks. Now the entire swamp was a minefield with timed charges.

Conrad brought his exo out of the swamp water and stamped on one of the remaining hives. The next hummock was only ten metres away. He got to it without any difficulty. The hive was small. He stamped it flat.

One left.

It was a big one; but he crushed it with his exo-hands. More fireworks. Sparks rising, fading, falling.

Conrad felt savagely glad. Now, the piranha bugs were virtually cleared from the potential colonization area.

158

Probably, there were other Piranha Bug Cities on the planet; but they could be dealt with by the people who would eventually tame Argus. Unless, of course, Kwango's baboons came to be classified as people . . . Meanwhile, the bridgehead had been established and secured.

Conrad stepped off the last hummock—and found that his exo was immediately in deep water. No matter. The water was not up to the control dome. The edge of the swamp was not more than thirty metres away. He started wading.

He made it about half-way to the edge of the swamp, then his left exo-foot got trapped between two huge submerged boulders. He tried to lift it, and couldn't. He tried to move backwards, and couldn't. He tried to move forwards, and couldn't.

"Matthew, how much time left till detonation?"

"Six minutes, seventeen seconds, sir. Do you have a problem?"

Conrad laughed grimly. "Yes, Matthew, I have a problem. One of my exo-feet has become wedged between two rocks. I can't free myself."

"Condition appreciated, Commander. Mark and I can enter the swamp and endeavour to remove the charges we have placed. Impossible to estimate time required for recovery, owing to lack of data on condition of sediment and other factors."

Conrad struggled frantically; but the exo-foot was jammed hard.

"Do not enter the swamp. I will unharness and try to swim or walk ashore. If I fail, supply Mr. Kwango with all relevant data."

Conrad unharnessed as rapidly as he could. Then he opened the exo-dome and jumped into the swamp water.

His coverall was waterproof; but the sensation was revolting. The swamp was alive with larvae. There must be hundreds of thousands of them, thought Conrad. The water glowed dully with their presence. He had jumped into the middle of a shoal.

He could feel the things wriggling all around him. Vaguely, he wondered if they had the same voracious capacity as the fully grown bug. He had his helmet on, so at least the bastard creatures couldn't get at his face. But the pressure of all those wriggling bodies on his suit was horrible. He didn't even know whether the movements were caused by sheer weight of numbers or whether he was being attacked. He cancelled the thought. There was no profit in that kind of speculation. Not if you wanted to stay sane.

But another dreadful factor was now involved. Despite the fact that Conrad was a good swimmer, he was steadily sinking. He knew why.

Before he had jumped out of the exo-dome, Conrad had sealed his suit and vizor, and had clipped on an emergency air-bottle.

The trouble was that the air-bottle was weighing him down. He had already sunk below the surface before he figured it out. Now, the wriggling swimming larvae were all over his vizor. He could see nothing but a myriad wriggling, glowing bodies.

His feet touched the bottom of the swamp. He could unclip the bottle. But, if he did so, would he be able to rise through the seething mass? And if he could not get topside, which way would he have to walk, or push himself? He had lost all sense of direction.

Also, if he unclipped the air-bottle, there would only be enough air in his suit to last maybe two minutes.

Also, the bloody seismic charges would be going off in about two minutes, anyway.

Also, he had no means now of contacting Matthew and somehow getting himself talked out.

Too many bloody alsos!

"Right, Conrad," he said softly. "You are in the shit. Don't just stand there. Jettison the bottle and start moving. Execute!"

But his hands wouldn't move.

"Jettison the bottle, you stupid bastard!" he sobbed. "That is an order. Execute!"

Somehow, he regained control of himself. He unclipped the bottle, and the automatic seal in the suit air-feed closed.

The loss of the air-cylinder was not enough to make him buoyant. He stayed on the swamp mud with the larvae swirling about him.

Then he got sensible. He used his prosthetic arm. With rapid beating motions—so rapid that his bio-arm could not keep up—he churned the swamp water and the larvae close to him into a forming mixture of water and crushed protoplasm.

He rose towards the surface like an atomically powered torpedo—which, indeed, he had become.

The timing was quite spectacular. As he broke the surface of the swamp, the seismic charges exploded.

The entire swamp erupted great spouts and fountains of water. With the force of his rise, Conrad was half out of the water before the first pressure wave hit him. It assisted his progress.

He was lifted clear of the swamp—blown six metres into the air by the force of the simultaneous explosions—and fell in a heap almost at Matthew's feet.

The vizor was shattered, the suit was torn to ribbons, and Conrad was mercifully unconscious.

Matthew ascertained that he was still living, then picked him up gently. Matthew called the *Santa Maria*. "Situation report: mission accomplished. Commander Conrad injured and unconscious, but not—repeat not—in danger. Respiration moderately good, pulse low, no significant loss of blood, preliminary examination indicates no bones broken, no major organs damaged. Preliminary examination also indicates minor flesh wounds and severe concussion. Situation report ends."

It was Kwango who answered. "Stay where you are, Matthew. I have a fix. Norstedt will get the hovercar and bring him in."

Phase Five

On the Receiving End

Conrad groaned and shuddered and ground his teeth. He was having a nightmare. A bad one. He was dreaming that he was back in the swamp and that the larvae had found a way into his suit and that he was drowning in the swamp water, and that the things were all over his face and even in his mouth and lungs as he gasped hopelessly for air.

He didn't hear the voice that tried to soothe him, or feel the hand that held his hand, or the cloth that was used to wipe the sweat from his dripping forehead.

He screamed dreadfully and was woken by the sound of his own voice. He opened his eyes instantly, tried to sit up, fell back. He was shaking and sweating and his heart was pounding and he felt awful.

But rationality returned. He saw Lieutenant Smith bending over him. White hair, brown face. Entirely beautiful.

He gave a great sigh. All his muscles relaxed. He knew where he was. Rapidly, he did a total recall.

"Was it bad?" she asked gently.

He gave a faint smile. "Bad enough . . . A nightmare . . . I dreamed the bloody larvae had—cancel statement!" He pulled himself together and sat up. "What the hell are you doing on your feet, Lieutenant? I gave orders that——"

"Lie down and relax, mister! That is an order."

Lieutenant Smith's voice held a note of command in it. Conrad did not feel inclined to argue. He sank back on his pillow.

"What the devil is going on around here?" he asked weakly.

"You have been out two days, James. I am now opera-

162

tional, you are not. I am now in command, you are not."
Her voice hardened. "And if there is any trouble from you,
spaceman, I'll shoot you full of sleep juice again. Understood?"

It had all happened before; but Conrad's mind was
not yet clear enough to recall where or when.

"Understood, Commander. Where is Kwango?"

"Here, Boss." The black man's face hovered over Conrad, displaying a toothy smile. "Ah did not wish to intrude
on dis touching little scene, but ah sho' am grateful dat
you should remember dis little ole nigra in a moment o'
crisis."

"Kurt, you black bastard, kindly belay that Uncle Tom
crap. I'm not feeling too good, but I can still use my prosthetic arm."

"Sorry, Boss. I'm trying to kick the habit. But this
situation is rapidly becoming a tradition."

Conrad looked at Lieutenant Smith. "What's the damage, Indira?"

Lieutenant Smith gazed at him severely. "You, spaceman, are nothing but a piece of human wreckage in a
sick bay. I suppose I should be grateful that you didn't
break any bones this time. But I'm not. Severe concussion,
massive bruising, some internal bleeding, superficial rup-
turing of blood vessels, minor flesh wounds—Conrad,
when it comes to proving new worlds, you have some very
nasty habits."

"Yes, love. What's the sentence this time?"

"Don't call me love. I am now in command of this ex-
pedition. Get that into your stupid head."

"Sorry, Commander. How long do you estimate that I
will be unfit for duty?"

"Three days if you're lucky."

Conrad sat up again. "Damnation, woman! I'm fit for
duty now."

"Four, five or six days if you don't co-operate," snapped
Indira relentlessly.

Conrad appealed to Kwango. "Kurt, get some sense into
this bloody woman. This is *my* show. I am not going to

163

lie on my backside while idiots like Robinson try to get themselves killed."

Kwango shook his head. "Boss, *you* tried to get yourself killed. Also, you wrecked a very expensive exo. And if you threaten me with your prosthetic arm again, I'll smash you right through your bed. Message ends."

"Kurt, you are a traitor."

"Yes, Boss."

"Lieutenant Smith, I am now in full possession of my faculties and——"

"Spaceman, you are buying trouble."

Conrad knew when he was beaten. "All right! All right! Will somebody please update me? What's been going on?"

Kwango spoke. "A good question, old sport. One: you smashed Piranha Bug City. But totally. The hives, you took out yourself, as you may recall. The larvae did not care too much about being blasted. And while you were having a free ride back to the *Santa Maria*, Matthew and Mark lasered the reeds so that any surviving larvae would have no place to go. That swamp is—to quote dear Gunnar—kaput."

"So, that is one item off the worry list . . . How about your baboons, Kurt? Are you making any progress?"

Kwango smiled complacently. "I always make progress. I have their language now—most of it. I can talk to them, but not for long because it hurts my throat."

"The question is: are they people?"

"I don't think so; but I'm not sure. They have rudimentary language; but so do some primates on Terra. They use tools; but so do some animals on Terra. They got primitive engineering skills; but the North American beaver, for example, has them licked hollow. Their social organization is less elaborate than that of Terran baboons; but their rituals are more sophisticated . . . I put a detailed report on your desk, in case you want to beam something back to U.N. . . . The real point is that I think they could *become* people, Boss, in maybe fifty or a hundred thousand years."

"In which case," said Conrad, "they're not my problem. I'll look at your report as soon as this harpy——" he

164

glanced at Lieutenant Smith "gets her claws out of me. But we are not going to lift off Argus because some bloody monkeys might take it into their heads to evolve in the far future . . . Anyway, stay with them, Kurt. I want to know as much as possible about them." He grinned. "Now, let's forget the official crap you've given me to pass on to U.N. What made you *really* decide they aren't people?"

Kwango shrugged. "They got a complicated programme, Boss. But it is only a programme. They don't do anything except exist. No creativity, no experimentation, no irrationality, no inspiration, no neurosis, no aggression, no nothing."

Kwango did not know it; but his complacency about the baboons was soon to be shattered.

Lieutenant Smith said: "That is enough talk for the time being, Conrad. We are going to get some food into you, and then you're going to rest. If you behave yourself, you can come down to the saloon for half an hour this evening."

"Damnation!" said Conrad.

Phase Six

One Mystery: Three Solutions

The following evening at dinner, Kwango made an announcement, the terrible significance of which would only be realized much later.

All the Expendables were present. Matthew, as usual, was monitoring the screens. Conrad, after a day of model behaviour, had been allowed out of the sick bay to take his first meal in company. He had taken his medicine, submitted without complaint to E.E.G., E.C.G., sphygmometer, blood tests, electro-massage, vision and hearing tests and muscular co-ordination routines. It was the quickest way, he realized, of getting himself passed fit for duty. It was the only way.

Lieutenant Smith had given him the results of her examination. On the credit side: heart sound, head sound, hearing sound. On the debit side: blood pressure up, haemoglobin down, slight impairment of bio-vision, coordination poor. Sentence: two more days of rest and relaxation. Also further tests. He knew better than to argue. It had happened before. He always lost.

Significantly, he was not allowed to wear uniform or sit at the head of the table. Just to remind him that he was out on parole.

Lieutenant Smith sat at the head of the table. When Conrad asked Mark to bring some more brandy, she cancelled the order.

Conrad sighed, but made no protest. Norstedt looked at him amazed. Mirlena Robinson stuck out her breasts and smiled insolently. Maeve O'Brien tried to conceal her amusement. Kwango enjoyed it all.

He pushed his plate away. "My, that was a mighty fine meal. Who dropped the beef?"

"I did," said Norstedt. "I voss trying to catch zis goddam big running bird for der zoo vile you vos playing mit your baboon friends. Stepped sadly on young bull rhino by mistake. Regrettable for rhino, not too bad for us, eh?"

Maeve O'Brien pushed her plate away. Norstedt laughed uproarishly. Conrad spoke, temporarily forgetting he was out on parole. "Norstedt, you are not empowered to go playing games in your exo when you are supposed to be chaperoning Kwango. You are fined one booze ration. You are a bloody fool. He could have been in trouble. He could have needed you fast."

"Sorry, Commander." Norstedt shrugged. "Dose baboons are very friendly. Dey play with Kwango and do him no harm."

"Nevertheless, you will carry out my orders. If I cannot rely on orders being obeyed, this mission will flounder."

"At the moment, Commander, you don't give orders around here." Lieutenant Smith's voice was mildly sarcastic. She felt that Conrad had been too rough on Norstedt.

Conrad glared at her. "I expect you to back me up, Lieutenant."

There was a brief, tense silence.

Kwango said hastily: "Talking of my baboons, Boss, I got an interesting little mystery. Some of them seem to have bad colds. They sneeze a bit and their eyes are weepy."

Conrad was interested. "Any other signs of change in their behaviour?"

"No."

"It doesn't seem much of a mystery."

"I think it is, Boss."

"Possible solutions," retorted Conrad. "One, it is some kind of infection which regularly hits them. Two, since you have been in close contact, you could have infected them . . . I read somewhere that when early explorers on Terra first made contact with the Eskimo, whole tribes were wiped out by being infected with the common cold—a bug they had never previously experienced." He grinned. "Let's hope it doesn't happen in this case, Kurt. U.N. does not approve of genocide."

"The reverse situation may apply," said Lieutenant Smith. "Their micro-organisms could knock us out. Kurt, as a precautionary measure, I want you to take two grammes of ascorbic acid daily and not to get too close to the infected animals."

"O.K., Lieutenant, if you say so." Kwango shrugged. "But I thought we had a prophylactic dose of vitamin C built into our normal diet."

"We do. Two hundred and fifty milligrammes. It is not enough for this kind of situation."

"There could be a third solution." It was Mirlena Robinson who spoke. She regarded Conrad with a superior smile, still sticking out her breasts in a kind of sexual challenge.

"Robinson," said Conrad irritably, "I have seen and handled better mammary glands than yours. You need not advertise the fact that you are female. It is apparent by your irrational behaviour. So far you have contributed

167

little to the success of this mission. Now, forget your hormones and get sensible. What is your third solution?"

Mirlena stood up, angry, breasts heaving. "I will not stay here to be insulted by a white racist . . . Kurt, you are black. Will you allow this—this white trash—to insult me?"

Kwango sighed. "Baby, I love you. But, like de good Commander says, in his own inimitable style, you are a shade impetuous. Cool it."

"You, too! You Uncle Tom!"

"Sit down, Robinson!" barked Conrad. "You have not been dismissed."

"You are no longer in command, Conrad," stormed Mirlena. "You got yourself smashed up. I take my orders from Lieutenant Smith."

"Then take them!" snapped Indira. "Sit down, Robinson. Answer *Commander* Conrad's question. We all know he lacks tact, but we bear with it. *He* has a record of delivering the goods . . . Now I am brown—not black, not white—but brown. And I am telling you that you are the only racist present. So sit down and answer his question or I will stamp you into a jelly."

Conrad was amazed. So was Kwango. So was Mirlena.

She sat down, weeping.

Presently, she recovered herself. "I apologize for my childish behaviour. Please forgive me." She glanced at Conrad nervously.

"I am sorry I said the things I said. Now what is your third solution?"

"Hay fever—or something analogous to hay fever. Has anyone noticed my pollen counter? I set it up outside the perimeter."

Conrad smiled. "That thing with a vane fixed so that the funnel always faces the wind? I thought someone was making some kind of met study."

"It is a private venture. I am rather interested in pollens . . . The machine is a simple device. The pollen carried on the wind is blown into the funnel and trapped on a fine gauze screen. So far, I haven't had much time to investigate the pollens; but I have noticed that the coun-

168

is rather heavy when the wind blows from the west."

"Interesting," said Conrad. "I hope you will continue the investigation. Keep me informed of any significant results."

Kwango smiled. "Nice work, Mirlena. So now we got three theories . . . To me, it looks as if the baboons have some kind of virus infection; but virology is not one of my subjects . . . Whatever the thing is, it doesn't seem to bother them too much. But I am puzzled. I, Kwango, am definitely puzzled. It had to happen."

Conrad said: "O.K., Kurt. I knew you were saving a punch line. What is it?"

"Only the males are infected," said Kwango.

"Are you sure, Kurt?" Lieutenant Smith sounded sceptical.

Kwango shrugged. "I'll rephrase it. All the females I saw were not showing any symptoms."

Conrad yawned, not knowing that his drink had been spiked. "Well, let me know if there is any change in their behaviour."

"Time for bed, Commander. You've had a busy day." Lieutenant Smith gave him a rather enigmatic smile. Conrad yawned again, too tired to notice.

"O.K., Commander. It looks as if I am a bit more beat-up than I thought. Good night, everyone."

He got to his feet a trifle unsteady, blinked and yawned again. Lieutenant Smith, knowing he was a very obstinate man, had given him the maximum dose.

Phase Seven

Kwango's Horror Show

It was a fine morning. Kwango and Norstedt were in good spirits. Kwango was secretly rather pleased about the mystery of the sneezing male baboons. He intended to

169

solve the problem before anyone else did. It would be good for his ego. Norstedt, also, had his own secret ambition. He was, by damn, going to catch one of those big running birds that could travel faster than an ·exo. While he had been "chaperoning" Kwango, he had noticed that several flocks of the birds seemed to favour the grasslands near the forest where the baboon colony was established. This time he would not rely upon speed—which didn't work— but upon cunning. He proposed to scoop out a pit with his exo-hands, camouflage it, then drive the birds towards it. He did not propose to tell Conrad.

They had taken breakfast early in the saloon. Conrad was not present. Lieutenant Smith's knock-out drops had assured him of a long, relaxed sleep without any more nightmares.

Lieutenant Smith was present at breakfast. Before Kwango and Norstedt left, she reminded them of Conrad's strictures.

"Kurt, you will be laser armed."

"Yes, ma'am. How is de good commander dis sunny day?"

Indira smiled faintly. "Sleeping it off, Kurt. I hit him with Nembutal."

Kwango grinned. "He is not going to like that too much if he ever finds out."

"But he won't ever find out, Kurt, will he?"

Kwango adopted his saintly expression. "Not from me, Lieutenant. It is on your conscience."

"Gunnar," said Lieutenant Smith, "don't go playing any more games. It is not good for the Commander's blood pressure. Stay with Kurt and monitor him. Commander Conrad may be difficult, but he knows more about taming planets than all the rest of us put together."

Norstedt regarded her with wide-eyed innocence. "I vill not play games, Mademoiselle Lieutenant. I haf der pluperfect regard for *mon capitaine*'s marbles."

When Norstedt had harnessed up, he stopped and lowered his interlock exo-fingers as a cradle for Kwango.

"Ver to, soldier?" Inside the exo, Norstedt had to use his transceiver.

"Follow that cab," replied Kwango, arranging himself comfortably on the massive exo-hands.

"Vot cab?" Norstedt was nonplussed.

"Any cab, stupid. Just make sure it leads to my baboons. Double fare if you make it in twenty minutes."

Norstedt cottoned on, having mentally translated the vernacular through three languages. "Ah, so. Iss yoke, no? It shall be, comrade samurai. You are there pronto."

It was Kwango's turn to be perplexed.

About half-way to the forest, the exo developed a slight fault. The left foot did not respond exactly to Norstedt's movements. It began to come down too heavily, the result being that Kwango was somewhat jolted.

"Cool it, you clumsy Swede! If you can't handle the exo, get out and leave it to the expert."

"Iss not mein fault, Kwango. Dere iss failure in simulation system, I stink. No matter, *mon brave*, I fix when we arrive."

"You stink," agreed Kwango. "Drop to 30 k.p.h. before you drop me or bust my spine. I hope you can fix it before it is time to go home. De good commander gaily wrecked one of these things when he was taking out the piranha bugs. He won't like it too much if we lose another."

"Not to worry, *mon vieux*. I fix. I know the circuitry of zees goddamn exos by heart."

A hundred metres from the forest, Norstedt gently deposited Kwango on the ground, laid the exo down and unharnessed. He came out of the control dome.

"Thank you for nothing," said Kwango. "That was a rough ride."

Norstedt shrugged. "Iss not my intervention. Relax, *soyez tranquille*, amigo. Go play mit der baboons. I fix before you have kittens. Hokay?"

"Hokay," said Kwango. "Your command of English is rapidly disintegrating into total anarchy, Gunnar. Interesting. I wonder why."

Norstedt was puzzled. "I fail to communicate?"

"No. You don't fail to communicate. But every time you speak, the message gets more garbled."

"*Wunderbar!*" said Norstedt happily. "You do me too

much honour. Have fun, friend of my youth. I fix vile you play mit der naughty monkeys. Not to worry, old son. All will be *de trop*."

"All is already *de trop*, Gunnar," remarked Kwango drily. "Just trace the fault and adjust the circuitry. I'll come back soon to see how you are getting along. Right?"

Norstedt gave a ceremonial salute. "Right, *Herr Ober-gruppenführer*. *Ganz gut!*"

Kwango gave him a despairing glance, checked his laser rifle, and went into the forest.

It was full of surprises. He came back to Norstedt and the exo far faster and far sooner than he had anticipated.

The baboon village was, apparently, deserted. The first thing Kwango registered was a dead baboon, male. Its arms had been torn off, and its head had been battered into pulp.

Kwango had the feeling that he was being watched. He glanced round him quickly—at the bases of the trees, at the tops of the trees. He could not see any animal life. But he still had the feeling of being watched.

He turned to go. A baboon launched itself from no-where. Kwango sensed rather than saw it coming. He side-stepped, and it went hurtling past him, its hard sharp nails raking his coverall in passing. He glimpsed the look of ferocity on its face and was astounded. It rolled over twice, picked itself up and came at him again. He lasered it. The animal still kept moving, even with a hole burned through its brain. Its dead body fell almost at his feet.

Kwango heard a noise and tried to turn. He was too late. One had either jumped or dropped from a tree and had clamped itself on to his back. The legs were locked in a agonizing scissor-grip round his waist, while the baboon was using its strong arms to force his head back and break his neck.

Instinctively, Kwango did the only thing it was possible to do. He fell backwards, heavily. There was an agonized grunt as nine-five kilos of black, muscular Nigerian knocked all the wind out of the animal as it hit the ground.

Its legs and arms briefly became rubber and it gulped convulsively for air. Kwango struggled free, grabbed his laser rifle and jumped up—just in time to meet another one coming at him. His aim was bad. He burned a hole through its chest, but it still came on as if it did not want to know. Hastily, he lasered its head. The air stank of burning flesh and bone.

The one behind him had recovered enough to try again. He swung only in time to knock it sideways with the barrel of the laser rifle. He burned it as it was picking itself up for a third go.

The stench of burning flesh made Kwango want to vomit. But there wasn't any time for luxuries.

Another baboon dropped out of a tree. It miscalculated, and landed a metre in front of Kwango. As it lunged, he kicked expertly at the jaw. He connected. The head snapped back, the spinal column was broken. The animal was dead on arrival. It slumped in a heap, clawing vainly at him in its last second of life.

Suddenly, the entire forest seemed to be alive with noises. Mindless roars of anger and hate. Not at all like the baboon sounds he had recorded and fed into the ship's computer.

Kwango had had enough. More than enough. There was only one place he wanted to be now, and that was elsewhere. Considerably elsewhere.

He turned and started to run out of the forest. Two more baboons dropped out of the trees and barred his path. He lasered one and took a flying kick at the other. He heard and felt ribs break as he connected. The baboon flopped back. Kwango did not stop to inspect the damage.

He ran out of the forest with a speed that would have been envied by any Olympic sprinter in the last two hundred years. For once, Kwango would not have been interested to know that he was breaking records. He just wanted out.

Now he was clear of the forest. He glanced back and saw that the baboons were still coming—about twenty of them, maybe more. Fortunately, they did not have his turn of speed. He was still gaining. About two hundred metres away on the grassland, Norstedt was tinkering with the exo, his back to Kwango.

While he was still running, Kwango managed to do some calculations. It would be about twenty-five seconds before the baboons got as far as the exo.

He wanted to warn Norstedt, and tell him to harness up. But he didn't have the breath. He tried to shout, but all that came out of his mouth was an agonized groan.

He had an idea. He stopped, turned and lasered the three leading baboons. The rest did not want to know. They came on. He could not laser them all. He started running again.

He was about twenty-five metres away from the exo, before Norstedt registered his presence and that of the pursuing baboons. The expression on his face was one of comical disbelief.

Kwango slowed enough to allow him to shout with bearable agony. "Get into the exo!" he screamed. "Harness up! I'll try to draw them away. Get that thing up and grab me as soon as you can."

Norstedt was shouting something; but Kwango could not hear. There was a pounding in his head and a great pain in his chest. He turned and bought three or four more seconds of precious rest by lasering the two nearest baboons. His aim was dreadful. He could hardly hold the laser rifle. He burned ground twice before he hit the baboons. He seared an arm off the leader; but that did not stop it. The arm fell grotesquely. The animal did not want to know. It came on, but more slowly.

He was luckier with the second baboon. The laser beam sliced it neatly in two. The torso fell, writhing. Kwango watched, fascinated, as the legs took three more steps before they, too, fell in a bloody, smoking heap.

The rest were coming on fast. Kwango did not waste time looking at what Norstedt was doing.

He made noises to keep the attention of the berserk animals and veered off to the right, hoping to lead them away from Norstedt and the exo.

Kwango ran until his legs turned to rubber and he sank to the ground. His vision was not too good, but his mind was still working. He rolled on to his stomach and faced his pursuers, laser rifle raised, but his arms were shaking as he sobbed for breath.

He was amazed to discover that only seven baboons were now pursuing him. He knew he was shaking all over, so he did his best to aim the rifle carefully. He lasered the leading baboon when it was only eight or nine metres away. Smoke and steam rose as the animal's brain was burned out of its head.

He caught the next two in a sweeping beam that severed their heads from their bodies.

Kwango gained heart. He stood up groggily and lasered the remaining four as they came at him, burning heads, chests, legs. The last one died almost at his feet, a charred and smouldering wreck.

He vomited. The vomit fell on what was left of the dead baboon's face and sizzled with the residual heat of the laser beam.

Kwango started thinking again. He had not taken out the entire troop. What had happened to the rest?

He gazed at the exo—and got his answer.

Norstedt's attempt to harness up had not been successful. The baboons must have registered his movements and divided their attack.

Now they were tearing his body to pieces.

Kwango forgot the taste of vomit in his mouth, forgot his fear, forgot his fatigue. With a great roar of anger, he rushed at the baboons. There were five of them. They were playing with what was left of Gunnar Norstedt as if they were taking apart an old rag doll.

They registered Kwango's approach. They became interested. Maybe it had penetrated their simian minds that Norstedt was not going to provide much more entertainment.

Kwango roared at them again. "Come on, you monkeys out of hell!" he sobbed. "Come and collect!"

The baboons obliged.

Kwango had the presence of mind to wait until they were clear of the exo and Gunnar's remains before he started burning.

For a minute or two, he went mad with bloodlust and sheer sadism.

He didn't laser to kill. He lasered only to maim, wound, inflict pain. Those creatures had to pay for what they had done to Gunnar. For starters, he burned a leg and an arm off the leading baboon and laughed as it tried to hop forward, smoking and steaming, spinning crazily. It fell down, screaming. The screams were like music.

The next one, Kwango blinded. It tripped over its dying comrade and proceeded—blindly—to attack it.

The remaining three were undaunted. Fear, pain, death, screams, the smell of burning flesh apparently meant nothing to them.

They came on.

Kwango became an artist in inflicting pain. He had stopped trembling now. He was no longer hot and sweaty. He was ice-cold. He wanted vengeance.

Expertly he burned the hands off one baboon. Then he burned off its feet. It still came crawling at him on the stubs of its limbs, crying dreadfully as its life's blood ebbed away.

The next one got special treatment. Kwango lasered its genitalia, then opened up its stomach so that its gut fell out. The baboon paused momentarily in bewilderment, then tried to stuff its intestines back where they belonged. It came on. The intestines fell out of the still smoking and steaming wound yet again. The baboon sat down and tried to work out what had happened. It died in the sitting position. Kwango laughed uproariously.

"What a swell party this is!"

The last baboon collected the *cordon bleu* treatment. Kwango notched his laser rifle down to low burn and roasted the animal alive. First, he sizzled off its hair. It danced. It danced grotesquely as he turned its skin into crackling. It screamed, so he roasted its mouth.

Obstinately, it refused to die. So first he roasted an arm, and was pleased to see hot fat spitting from the well-cooked flesh. The baboon convulsed, but somehow it still stayed on its feet. So Kwango cooked a leg.

The baboon hopped about for two or three seconds. Then it died in mid-hop. Kwango was disappointed.

He stood quite still, as if frozen, for several minutes,

staring at nothing, feeling nothing. Then he shook himself out of the trance, and made an effort to get rational. He walked slowly towards the exo, slowly realizing the true horror of the situation. It did not lie in the dreadful carnage around him. It lay in the terrible fact that, for a few nightmarish minutes, he had behaved like a sadistic maniac.

Kwango had dropped his own transceiver somewhere. He didn't know where, and it didn't matter. He would have to use the one in the exo. And that meant he would have to step over the remains of Gunnar Norstedt.

He tried hard not to see what had happened to Gunnar, but he couldn't avoid it. He was sick again.

Somehow, he got to the exo transceiver. By which time, he was shaking and crying. But that old Kwango pride made him calm down a little before he radioed.

"Calling *Santa Maria*. Come in *Santa Maria*."

Matthew answered. Good old Matthew! Superior Matthew. A robot. Not a human being. A robot. And robots could not go mad.

"I read you, Mr. Kwango. Please proceed."

Tears were streaming down Kwango's face. "Get a fix on me, Matthew."

"Decision noted. Execution proceeds."

"Now hook me up to Commander Conrad."

"Commander Conrad is in sick bay, sir."

"I forgot. Get Lieutenant Smith."

Indira's voice next. "What is it, Kurt? Are you in trouble?"

"Lovely Lieutenant, you could say with some accuracy that I am in trouble." Kwango tried to sound flippant and failed. "Get the chopper here fast and lift me out."

"What has happened, Kurt?"

Kwango laughed. It was hysterical laughter. He knew it. Indira knew it. "Too long to explain, dear lady. The baboons went crazy, Norstedt is dead, I am a monster. *Please* lift me out."

"Hold it, Kurt. I'm on my way."

Matthew's voice next. "E.T.A. chopper, Mr. Kwango, seven minutes plus or minus————"

"I know," said Kwango, wearily. "You are lucky, Matthew. You are not mad, you are not sane, you can't cry. You are entirely logical. Over and out."

Presently, the chopper came down out of the sky. Lieutenant Smith stepped out of it and ran towards the exo.

Kwango was leaning against the exo-skeleton. He was not looking at anything in particular, he was not doing anything in particular. He was just humming to himself discordantly: Swing low, sweet chariot.

Lieutenant Smith saw what had happened to Norstedt. She, too, was sick.

"Welcome to de clan," said Kwango tranquilly. "I trust you bring tidings of comfort and joy."

Indira wiped the vomit from her mouth. "Can you make it to the chopper, Kurt?"

"That is a question, and a question requires some thought before it is answered. Simplify the problem, Lieutenant. Make it an order."

She realized he was in shock. "Move, Kwango!" she shouted. "Get into the chopper, you black bastard!"

Kwango grinned. "Now that is the language I understand."

He walked drunkenly towards the chopper.

He almost made it. Then he fell flat on his face.

Somehow, Lieutenant Smith pulled him aboard and lifted off.

Kwango recovered his wits a little before the chopper touched down by the *Santa Maria*.

He was not aware that he had sneezed twice. Lieutenant Smith was too busy taking the chopper back at top speed to notice.

Phase Eight

Conrad Sneezes

Conrad said: "Where's Kwango, Lieutenant?"

"In his cabin. I don't think he is ready to face anybody yet."

"I'll decide about that."

"You won't decide anything," snapped Indira. "You are still my patient."

"I hereby declare myself fit for duty. I am resuming command."

"You are not!" she stormed. "You will resume command when I judge you to be fit."

Conrad stood up. "You are wasting your time and mine. Don't try to stop me leaving the sick bay."

"I could make a mess of you, spaceman." She slapped her tin legs. "So don't try anything."

Conrad smiled and raised his prosthetic arm. "Interesting. We trained in the same school, love. We have lost two men—both, as far as I can see, through negligence. If I have to kill you to regain command, I will. But that would leave us three down. Not good."

Indira was aghast. "You would, too! What kind of man are you, James Conrad?"

Conrad put on his uniform. Not his coverall. His uniform.

"You know what kind of man I am, Lieutenant Smith. I am a bastard. I only know how to get things done—my way . . . Argus has already cost us. Maybe it will cost us some more. We both face a tribunal of the dead—our own, and those who starved to give us the chance to prove this planet. I intend to prove Argus. The thought of people dying needlessly offends me. Argus may stop me, but nothing else will. Do I pass by you or over you, Lieutenant Smith?"

Suddenly, Indira was crying. "Oh, James, we are both idiots. But you are right. You know how to get things done. But you are killing yourself—do you know that?"

He kissed her, held her briefly. "Cool it, Lieutenant. See to the ladies. Give Maeve and Mirlena an edited version of what happened. Understood?"

Indira wiped the tears from her face. "Understood . . . James, I am glad you won the trial of strength. I am not programmed for command decisions. It's your party."

Conrad gave a faint smile. "There would not have been a struggle, love. It would have been too messy for both of us." He opened his prosthetic hand, and revealed what he had been holding. It was a medal. The Grand Cross of Gagarin, which he had been awarded for services rendered on Kratos. "This would have hit you hard enough to stop you, no more."

"James, I love you."

Conrad tossed the medal on the sick bay bed. "Send a bottle of booze to Kwango's cabin. Scotch, vodka, brandy. It doesn't matter."

"Medically speaking," said Indira, "Kurt is in no state to ingest alcohol."

"The hell with clinical diagnosis," said Conrad. "Send a bottle. He needs it, I need it. O.K.?"

Lieutenant Smith smiled and saluted. "O.K., Commander."

*   *   *

Kwango was curled up in the womb position on his bunk. He did not pay any attention when Conrad came into the cabin. He was humming to himself: Swing low, sweet chariot.

"Hello, Kurt. I hear you've had a hard day."

No response.

The robot Luke brought the booze and the glasses. Conrad was glad that Lieutenant Smith had ordered Scotch. It looked like it was going to be a whisky session.

180

He waited till the robot had left, then he tried again.

"Kurt, you have seen nasty things in the woodshed before. Tell it like it was. I want to know."

Still no response.

Conrad sighed. He poured himself some whisky. A large dose. He drank it."

"Kwango, you lousy Nigerian shit, get up when you are addressed by a superior officer. So your ego is hurt. It doesn't bother me. Tell me what happened or I'll chop you into pieces!"

The message got through. Kwango uncurled, got out of his bunk, flopped groggily on to a chair.

He gazed at Conrad blearily. "It's bad, Massa Boss."

Conrad poured him a quadruple scotch. "Drink that, stupid. You don't deserve it, but drink it."

Kwango swallowed about half of it, and then told his story, omitting none of his maniacal actions.

"That's the way it was, Boss. I've flipped. I have gone over the hill. My best advice to you is to stick me in the cooler."

"When I need your advice, I'll ask for it," snapped Conrad. "Drink some more whisky. That is an order."

Kwango smiled faintly and held out his glass. "Some of your orders are easier to obey than others."

Conrad filled both glasses.

"I just remembered," said Kwango. "You're supposed to be in the sick bay."

"I discharged myself and resumed command."

Kwango gazed at him wonderingly. "How did you get past de good Lieutenant?"

"I offered to spread her all over the bulk-head if she didn't get out of the way." Conrad sipped his whisky tranquilly.

Kwango laughed. "And I had to miss dat little confrontation. It's not my day . . . Boss, you are a very hard man."

"I know."

Kwango raised his glass and drank deeply. "So where do we go from here, Boss? There has to be other colonies of those crazy baboons around. I'm not thinking too well,

181

but I think we got problems."

"Kurt, our mission is simple——to prove that man can survive on this planet. If we can secure and hold a colonization area, the colonists themselves will expand it. We are going to secure the colonization area." Conrad took another swig of whisky and promptly sneezed. Tears came to his eyes. He wiped them away on the back of his hand.

Kwango was suddenly alert. "Boss, you just sneezed. The first symptom in those baboons was——"

"Shut up!" snapped Conrad irritably. He scratched his silver eye-patch. "You are a nervous wreck, Kurt. Understandable after what you have been through . . . Some of the bloody whisky went down the wrong way, that's all."

Kwango shrugged. "Sorry, Boss. I'm on edge."

"As I was saying," went on Conrad. "We have to secure the colonization area and give it a twenty-four carat guarantee. So we use all available means——chopper, hovercar, exos, robots——to find out where other baboon colonies exist. Then we set up another study programme and see if we can find out what makes them go crazy."

"And if we can't?" asked Kwango.

"Then, we take them out," said Conrad ruthlessly. "You yourself said they weren't people. If they aren't people, they can bloody make room for people. Terra has too many people. That is why we are here."

Kwango put his glass down. "Boss, I don't much care for your attitude. You took out those purple mushrooms, you took out the harpoon trees and you took out the piranha bugs. Seems to me, you are out to wreck the entire ecology of Argus. That is madness."

"*You* talk to me about madness!" Conrad poured more whisky into both glasses. "Drink up, Kurt, and get sensible. We are going to give Argus a new eco-system, that's all. The planet is suitable for colonization. I don't care too much about indigenous life-forms. I do care about my own kind. If I have to wipe out half the flora and fauna of Argus to make it fit for human beings, I'll do it."

Kwango stood up, swaying a little, and threw his glass on the deck. It shattered. The whisky ran in tiny rivulets.

"Conrad, your attitude is monstrous. You are paranoid. You can't play God."

Conrad stood up also. "Can't I, Kurt? Every time we come to an E-type planet, I have to play at being God. I don't like it, but that's the way it is. I have to command. I have to make decisions. That's the way it is."

"You are a fascist," said Kwango thickly.

"I don't understand the term. Explain. Amplify."

"You are a Nazi."

"I still don't understand. Explain. Amplify."

Kwango lost his cool. "Your historical knowledge is zero, Massa Boss, Commander, sir. But Mirlena was right. You are a white racist pig. Does that connect?"

Conrad smiled. "It connects. Good night, Kurt. You are going to sleep. Tomorrow, we will devise a programme for a search and study and/or destroy strategy for other baboon colonies. Sleep well."

"I don't feel sleepy at all," said Kwango.

"You will," said Conrad. In a blur of movement, his prosthetic fist hit Kwango's jaw. The timing and the force applied were excellent. Nothing broken.

As Kwango sagged, Conrad caught him and lifted him on to his bunk.

Conrad sneezed.

"Damnation!" said Conrad.

Phase Nine

All the Colours of Nightmare

Conrad was up early; but Kwango was up earlier. There were signs of his passing in the saloon.

Maeve O'Brien, half-naked, half-conscious, bruised, beaten and very obviously raped lay moaning on the deck.

Conrad sneezed, bent down, lifted her head. "Kwango?" It was more of a statement than a question.

"I tried to stop him," she mumbled painfully. "He said something about saving Argus from white racist plunderers . . . He was out of his mind."

Mirlena Robinson came into the saloon. She gazed at the scene, horrified. "My God, Conrad! What have you done?"

Conrad sneezed again, forgot about Maeve, slammed her head back on the deck angrily and almost absentmindedly. She passed out.

Conrad stood up. Hazily, he was trying to work it all out. His mind would not function too well, but that was because he was tired.

Two facts connected: Kwango black, Robinson black. Maybe there was a plot. Maybe? Certainly! It fitted.

"I didn't rape her, Robinson. You know who raped her."

Mirlena came forward. "If you didn't rape her, Commander, sir," she said, "why the hell did you just bang her head on the deck and knock her out again. So she couldn't speak? You'll have to do better than that. You'll have to kill her. You'll have to kill all of us." She gave a grim smile. "This is the end for you, Conrad. You can't take us all out. You'll end up on a funny farm."

Conrad leaped at her, smashing her against the bulkhead. "Where is he, Robinson? You are in this with him. You are trying to set it up for him. Where is he?"

Conrad's bio-arm was across her throat, pinning her to the bulk-head. "I don't . . . know what . . . you are talking about," she gasped painfully. "You *are* mad!"

She tried to bring her knee up into his groin. Conrad laughed. He was there first. Mirlena grunted with pain and tried to double up. The hand across her throat pressed her harder against the bulk-head.

"Marks for effort, sweetie. Where is he?"

Mirlena was slowly choking. She clawed vainly at his arm, but could not move it.

Conrad tried another tactic. He lifted his prosthetic arm, grabbed at her coverall and tore it open from neck to crotch. He grabbed her breast with his prosthetic arm. "You and Kwango are plotting a take-over," he said softly. "I am going to do to you what he did to Maeve. Then I am going to kill him." He took his arm from her throat and, still holding her by the breast, threw her on to the deck.

Mirlena's head hit hard. Conrad leaped on her, prepared to silence her if necessary. It wasn't necessary. She was just gasping for air and trying to stay conscious. He gripped her breast with one hand and fumbled at his own coverall with the other. It was the prosthetic hand that gripped her breast. Mirlena's back arched with pain.

"Conrad, what the hell are you doing?" It was Lieutenant Smith's voice.

Conrad leaped to his feet and whirled to face her. "Kwango and Robinson are conspiring to destroy me and this mission. Take Robinson into custody, Lieutenant." He sneezed. "I'll deal with her when I have found Kwango."

"James, you are sick—very sick . . . Please come with me."

Conrad was appalled. "You, too, you brown bitch! You are in with them!"

Before Indira could react, Conrad's prosthetic arm shot out. The fist took her squarely on the chin. She fell in a heap.

Mirlena was trying to sit up. Conrad smiled and hit her. She fell back unconscious.

He tried to revive Maeve. He slapped her face gently. Presently, her eyes opened. "Don't worry, little one. You've had a rough deal." He sneezed. "I have to leave you and deal with Kwango before he gets up to any more mischief." He gestured towards the unconscious forms of Lieutenant Smith and Mirlena Robinson. "These are his accomplices. When you feel well enough, have them locked up."

Maeve tried to say something. But before she could, he let her head fall back and stood up.

Before Conrad was clear of the vessel, Lieutenant Smith had recovered consciousness and had alerted Matthew.

Conrad had a laser rifle. Peter and Paul attempted to stop him in the compound. He lasered their vision circuits.

Then, laughing insanely, he ran out of the compound. The sun was rising in a blue sky. It was a fine day for a hunt. A good day for a kill.

*   *   *

With insane logic, Conrad knew that Kwango would not be lurking in the vicinity of the *Santa Maria*. With insane logic, he knew that Kwango would be heading south— back to his beloved baboons. Maybe, he would try to enlist their help for the take-over. An interesting thought!

Conrad had completely forgotten about the previous day's massacre. All that mattered to him was that he should find Kwango and destroy him.

He felt good, but he felt strange. He felt immensely strong, omniscient, all-powerful. He didn't need a laser rifle to wipe out a pitiful thing like Kwango. It was a task better accomplished with his own god-like hands. He threw the laser rifle away and laughed, feeling in his imagination those god-like hands choking the black man slowly and horribly.

He ran, feeling no fatigue. Why should he feel any fatigue? He was god-like, immortal.

Oddly, Kwango, also, was heading south. Oddly, he, too, had forgotten about the previous day's massacre. Oddly, his insane logic was exactly like Conrad's.

Conrad was mildly interested when the sky turned gold and the grass turned black. He thought it was an aesthetic improvement. Then he reflected that it was a bad idea to have the grass black, because Kwango could hide in it.

Good thinking!

He willed the grass to turn pink. It instantly obliged. He decided that the sky would be better white, too, so that if that black bastard got himself on a skyline . . .

Obediently, the sky became white. Conrad was gratified. It was good to know that Argus respected his infinite power.

Conrad grew thirsty. He invented a stream, cupped his hands, drank some of the water. He felt refreshed. He cancelled the stream. It had served its purpose.

He hurried on. He willed his legs to go faster; and they went faster.

The sky turned blue again, and the grass became green.

"Does it matter?" asked Conrad aloud.

He decided that it didn't, but made a mental note to use other colours if he got bored.

He thought of Kwango—the lying, deceitful, treacherous Kwango. The black rapist! The monkey lover!

It was good, thinking of Kwango. It made the blood in his veins feel like liquid fire. It made him burn with a god-like desire for vengeance.

Conrad sped on. And presently, he caught sight of Kwango.

The black man was sitting on a grassy knoll, waiting for him.

"Hi, Boss," said Kwango pleasantly. "I knew you would come. And now you ain't going to do no more harm, because I'm going to take you out. You make like God, Boss. But you are just a cheap white power-drunk racist."

"Kwango, whatever I do to you, I am going to do slowly. I want to enjoy it," retorted Conrad.

Kwango leaped as he was speaking. Conrad was surprised. Being god-like, he had planned the encounter differently.

The two men fell over, rolling down the side of the knoll. Conrad was interested to note that the grass kept changing colour—pink to yellow to red. He hadn't planned that.

He managed to hit Kwango with his prosthetic fist. Not too hard.

Kwango, with smashed lips, skilfully rolled away, gasping for breath.

"The grass keeps changing from pink to yellow to red," complained Conrad. "Are you trying to be funny?"

Kwango picked himself up. So did Conrad.

"The grass is blue," snarled Kwango. "It's been blue all morning, except for a time when it was white. You always were stupid, Conrad."

With lightning speed, he delivered the famous Kwango head-butt. Conrad should have anticipated it, but he was

187

too busy being god-like. The negro head hit the Caucasian head—and won. Conrad swayed, saw purple stars in a green sky. Then he fell. Vaguely he wondered if his god-like plans were coming unstuck.

He opened his eyes. The grass had turned green again. Interesting.

Kwango loomed over him, gloating triumph on his black bestial face. He held a rock in both hands. He was going to smash it down on Conrad's head. Kwango brought the rock down with all his force.

Conrad's prosthetic arm blurred into action, smashing the rock sideways out of Kwango's hands. Conrad rolled in the same direction, grabbed the rock, stood up. He smiled. With the power in his arm he could make the rock travel with the speed and accuracy of a cannonball.

"Start running, Kwango," he taunted. "I'll give you a hundred metres—unless you want to go on your knees and beg for more."

Kwango had turned white.

"And don't change colour without my permission," snapped Conrad. "It is very annoying."

Kwango laughed. "You, Conrad, are yellow. You always were. That's why you need a tin arm . . . Toss your little boulder and see what happens—yellow trash!"

With a cry of rage, Conrad raised his prosthetic arm, ready to hurl the rock that would smash Kwango's head into jelly.

He heard a phut, and felt a stinging sensation in his back.

He paid no attention.

But just as he was about to throw the rock, the world went black.

There was another phut.

Kwango looked at his chest. His knees buckled.

At least, he and Conrad had found the some colour. It was a special kind of black called oblivion.

Final Phase

Who Did What and with Which and to Whom?

Conrad opened his eyes. He was in sick bay again. Kwango lay on a bunk beside him. He was awake.

Lieutenant Smith, Mirlena Robinson and Maeve O'Brien were present. Each of them had anaesthetic guns. Two were pointed at Conrad, one at Kwango.

"Welcome aboard," said Lieutenant Smith. "I don't think either of you are going to be able to play tennis for a while. But if you move that prosthetic arm, Conrad, you will go right back to sleep." She tapped her anagun significantly. "Understood?"

"Understood, Lieutenant."

"Commander, to you spaceman!"

"Sorry . . . Commander."

"How do you feel?"

"Lousy. Weak as a kitten."

Indira smiled. "So you should be. You have both been out for seventeen days. You have been fed intravenously, you have each had a seventy-five per cent blood change, almost every antibiotic known to man, and enough tranks to knock out an army." Then she added nastily: "Oh, I almost forgot. You both had a special present from Mirlena. She shot you full of simulated female hormones." Indira was enjoying herself. "You will be interested to know that your facial hair stopped growing and you both began to develop sweet little breasts. Then we relented and gave you back your manhood. Say thank you."

Conrad tried to sit up. It was no use. He had no strength.

"What the hell is going on around here?" He meant to roar, but his voice sounded weak and frail. He felt foolish.

189

Kwango spoke. "Boss, either we made a mess of things, or Women's Lib has taken over the mission."

"What the hell is Women's Lib?" Conrad was not too strong on twentieth-century social history. He was gratified to know that Kwango's voice sounded as weak as his own.

Kwango sighed. "Forget it, Boss. Fasten your seat-belt. They are going to tell us something we would rather not know."

Indira gazed at them incredulously. "You mean to say you don't remember?"

"Remember what!" snapped Conrad.

"What happened."

"Of course I remember wha happened! Kurt had a bad time with those bloody baboons. Norstedt got smashed, and you lifted Kurt out by chopper. That reminds me. Did you recover the exo?"

"Yes, we recovered the exo. Your memory is not too good, spaceman. What else happened?"

Conrad grinned faintly. "I pronounced myself fit for duty, Lieutenant. You may recall the circumstances."

"I do. What else happened?"

"Last night, I managed to get Kurt sensible with the aid of a bottle of whisky and some fatherly nonsense. Then we both went to bed."

"Last night—*that* last night—was seventeen nights ago."

"I see," said Conrad weakly, wondering if he ought to believe her. "Did somebody poison the whisky?"

Maeve spoke. "No, Commander. The whisky was O.K. It just happened that on the following morning, one of you beat me up and raped me. Then the other one beat me up some more."

"And it just happened," added Mirlena, "that when I came into the saloon and saw what was going on, one of you hit me, tried to tear off my clothes and do a repeat performance."

"Also," added Indira, "when *I* tried to intervene, one of you knocked me cold."

Conrad was appalled. Kwango was appalled. Conrad looked at the three women. Somehow, he knew that what they said had the ring of truth. He glanced at Kwango.

Kwango didn't look too happy. So he believed it as well!

"Who did what to whom?"

"Work it out for yourselves, gentlemen." Lieutenant Smith seemed to be enjoying the situation.

"Is that all?" asked Conrad weakly.

"No, that is not all. When you had finished being real tough with the ladies, you both headed south and then tried to kill each other. Mistakenly, perhaps, one of us followed you in the hovercar and put you both to sleep before you could succeed."

"Oh, my Gawd!" said Kwango.

Conrad made a great effort to pull himself together. He could feel the beads of sweat forming on his forehead, and he knew he didn't have much time. He gazed at Indira.

"So Kwango and I are washed up. You have recorded this information in the log, I presume. We will stand trial when we get back to Terra . . . Goddammit, woman, haven't you any good news?"

Indira Smith put down her anagun. "Concerning what, James?"

He tried to scratch his silver eye-patch, but was too weak. "Concerning Argus, woman! I don't matter, Kwango doesn't matter. Argus does . . . And don't call me James. It is bad for discipline, Commander."

Indira glanced at Mirlena and Maeve. The three women smiled at each other.

Indira spoke. "The good news is that we have proved the colonization area. Mirlena identified the agent that drove all those male baboons—and you male baboons—crazy."

"Not pollen," said Kwango weakly. He had been thinking.

"Yes, pollen, Kurt . . . Ever heard of L.S.D.?" asked Mirlena.

"A popular twentieth-century hallucinogen, I think, used by social drop-outs."

Mirlena smiled. "Score one. Lysergic acid diethylamide, derived from ergot, a poisonous, purplish fungus. It is colourless, odourless, tasteless. One gramme is sufficient to totally disorientate ten thousand people . . . I found a pollen that carried the same derivative as L.S.D. I traced the plant. It is something like the Terran mandrake. There were not many of them. They were easily identified because of the bones of dead animals in their vicinity. We took them out."

"Also," added Indira, "Maeve developed the antidote, for which you two male baboons may be grateful . . . We found two more colonies of local baboons, and we gave all the surviving males shots. Prognosis good. Colonization area proved."

Conrad sighed. "They don't need us, Kurt. We've had it. This is the planet that stopped us. You and I are obsolete. And all because of a bloody pollen! The next team will be composed entirely of women."

Indira bent over and kissed him on the lips. So did Mirlena Robinson. So did Maeve O'Brien.

Then each of them kissed Kwango.

Indira said: "You can both begin remedial exercises tomorrow."

Conrad tried to sit up again. It was not a good idea.

"Who raped whom?" he cried desperately.

"Spaceman," said Indira, "that is one thing we women are all agreed upon. Unless you can work it out for yourselves, you will never know."

Kwango said. "Boss, we are in the shit."

Conrad smiled. "We are taming Argus—correction, they are taming Argus—that is all that matters."

"Goddam women," said Kwango.

"Amen," said Conrad, and went tranquilly to sleep.